MISS
SOPHISTICATED
BITCH

By

Riiva Williams

Copyright © 2015 by *Marvelous Leaders Publications*

Published by Marvelous Leaders Publications LLC

Join our Mailing list by texting Marvelous at 95577

Facebook: Author Riiva Williams

This novel is a work of fiction. Any resemblances to actual events, real people, living or dead, organizations, establishments or locales are products of the author's imagination. Other names, characters, places, and incidents are used fictitiously.

Cover Design: Michael Horne

Editor: Kendra Littleton

Because of the dynamic nature of the Internet, any Web addresses or links contained in this book may have changed since publication, and may no longer be valid. The views expressed in this work are solely those of the author and do not necessarily reflect the views of the publisher and the publisher hereby disclaims any responsibility for them.

ACKNOWLEDGEMENTS

Thank you to Michael Horne for the awesome work that you do for the cover of this book.

Thank you to my editor Kendra Littleton. Thanks for your great work and I look forward to working with you again in the future.

Thank you to my mom for her countless bouts of encouragements whenever I set out to write a new book.

Thank you to Lenny Harris for being one of the rocks in my life. Whenever I need the encouragement to go on and advice on what to do it is you I come to.

EXCERPT

"So…. Where are you off too?" He had this smoothness about him I had to admit.

"I am heading home! It's my early day and I need to relax, so I can go over my notes for the Swartzman's case." Hoping that will detour him, I turned back to my office with him on my heels like a little puppy.

"Are you going to invite me over?" His smile melted my insides.

"No… No, I'm not." I glared at him praying he would take a hint and just go, so I can regroup.

Before I knew, it my door was closed and I was backed into a corner. I felt like a mouse that was just caught eating from the cheese and had nowhere to run. "Oh so you are one of those huh?" His smile turned menacing as he stepped closer.

"What? What are you talking about? What are you doing?" By now, I am pinned between his rock hard chest and the wall.

"There is no one here, I already checked and my dad just left to meet another client."

"So… that is supposed to move me? Now, move out of my way, so I can leave." I pushed at him but he did not budge. It was almost as if he was calculating his next move.

He laughed. It was so genuine that it made his eyes sparkle and all. "Miss Sophisticated Bitch alright.

Want to play all high and mighty acting as if she is not human like the rest of us. A human with needs… you haven't changed one bit Emma."

Before I thought it through properly, the slap sounded out in my office. Breathing heavily the tears stung my eyes. Still in shock, I was able to push him away from me. Walking to my chair where my things were he grabbed onto my hand and pulled me back into the corner, crushing his mouth on mines.

Dedicated to my crazy sisters nothing but all love Kris, Shelly and Abbi. This book is also dedicated to my son; you give me reason to keep on writing.

Chapter 1

My name is Emma Ross and to tell the truth, many people do not like me. Why? Just because I do not stand for the bullshit. It is that simple and it does not stop me from going about my life.

I have an active dating life, sort of.

I go out with friends every weekend. Oh wait, nope do not have those either.

I have an awesome sex life. With myself.

Ok, whom am I kidding? My life sucks. Sitting at my desk at *Regales and Ports*, I looked around at the available bachelors, so to speak, that were coming in and out of the law firm. There were many handsome young men that seemed ready to take on the world if I asked them too, but I was still skeptical on what passes through my coochie.

As I sat staring off into space, this fine ass brother walked in and my Spidey senses were at an all-time high. Scanning his six-foot frame from head to toe, my mouth began to water. He walked passed my door straight into Mr. McKinney's office.

I panicked a little bit because that meant I was having nasty thoughts about Junior! Taking in a mental note, I tried to erase the thought of having him lay my ass out in front of the fireplace at home.

Wow! I have not seen Jerome McKinney since high school, so that make one…two…three…four…FIVE years! He definitely came a long way from the goofy big-eared kid we all knew.

Sighing, I shook the image from my memory and continued working on the Progress Report for my team. I was just about finished when my name boomed over the intercom. Checking myself in my computer screen quickly, I crossed the hall to the boss' office.

"You called sir?" my voice broke a little bit because I was nervous.

"Don't look so nervous sit down, sit down!" he waved me to an empty chair that was right next to

Jerome. "Emma, this is my son Jerome. He will be helping you finish close out the Swartzman's case, which I would like done by the end of next week."

Holding out my hand to shake his, I saw the sexual appreciation in his eyes as he looked me over. My day's events just became more interesting. I turned back to Mr. McKinney Sr. as he finished his rant about getting everything in on time, so we can nail the bastard. His words not mine. I felt heated to the core, as Junior's gaze never wavered from me.

Five minutes later, I was safely behind my desk. Checking my clock, I saw that it was 5:30 pm. I quickly finished off my report and printed it, so I can leave to go home. Just as I placed the report in the tray for my boss to review, out pops Mr. Sunshine.

"So, where are you off too?" he had this smoothness about him, I had to admit.

"I am heading home! I get off early today and I need to relax, so I can go over my notes for the Swartzman's case," I hope that will detour him, as I turned back to my office. He was on my heels like a little puppy.

"Are you going to invite me over?" His smile melted my insides.

"No… No, I'm not," I glared at him, praying he would take a hint go, so I can regroup.

Before I knew it, my door was closed and I was backed into a corner. I felt like a mouse that was just caught eating the cheese and had nowhere to run. "Oh so, you're one of those, huh?" His smile turned menacing as he stepped closer.

"What? What are you talking about? What are you doing?" By now, I was pinned between his rock hard chest and the wall.

"There is no one here. I already checked and my dad just left to meet another client."

"So… that is supposed to move me? Now move out of my way, so I can be one of those people to leave." I pushed at him, but he did not budge. It was almost as if he was calculating his next move.

He laughed. It was so genuine it made his eyes sparkle. "Awe, come on, don't be a bitch alright? Trying to play all high and mighty acting as if you are not human like the rest of us. A human with needs... you haven't changed one bit, Emma."

Before I thought it through properly, the slap sounded off in my office. Breathing heavily, the tears stung my eyes. I could not believe that is what he thought of me. Still in shock, I was able to push him away. Walking to my chair, where my things were, he grabbed onto my hand and pulled me back into the corner, crushing his mouth on mine with a deep growl.

At first, I tried to fight him off, but my battle was with my raging hormones at this point. He took control and gently coaxed me pulling me deeper within his web. His fingers were making electric circles on my side and I sucked at self-restraint, as my womanhood started to seep her lovely juices from my core.

Slowly, he ran his hand up my thighs and hooked onto my lace panties that were soaked. Testing the waters to see the amount of control I still had, he glided a finger over the slippery entrance of my core. I groan and he plunged his finger into the heat.

I was lost and he knew he had me. Detaching himself from my lips, he lifted me up while still fingering me and carried me to the empty love seat. Pressing upward and rubbing on my clit, I moaned.

"I want to taste you Emma; your scent is driving me crazy," the only response I could make was a strangled sound, as he withdrew his magic hand and ripped my draws.

Jerome hiked my fashionable Bebé skirt above me hips and dove in for the kill. I could not take it no more and I had not even gotten the dick yet. As he ate as if it was his last meal, he made himself at home in between my legs. I spiraled higher at the feelings he was evoking to my body. Just as I was on the brink, he plunged two fingers into my pussy and worked my G-spot.

Higher and higher, I soared over the edge. At this point, I saw nothing but bright lights and stars. Slowly, he eased back and watched me. I was embarrassed to tell the truth. I was not expecting that type of reactions behind it. He was now grinning like a Cheshire cat and it kind of motivated me to show my skills off.

Getting up, I kicked off my Prada heels and knelt before him, his smile broadened even more, as he realized what I am about to do.

"It's not as bad as you think, right?" I debated with myself whether I should answer.

"It's not my choice of where I would want to be having sex, but I can work it out," I gave him a side glance as I unzipped his zipper and let his manhood spring free. Nine inches of hot chocolate ready to melt in my mouth. I almost came on myself just looking at it.

Sliding my tongue from the base of his rigid shaft towards the sensitive tip, I tasted the saltiness of his pre cum. Slowly; I began to work my magic repeatedly, until I saw his eyes rolled back in ecstasy.

"Oh shit Emma!" He pulled on my hair; yes, of course it is real, for all those thinking that black women cannot grow long hair.

I eased up a little and told him to watch me in my eyes. Slowly, I relaxed my throat and swallowed that shit completely. Coming up for air, he pulled me into his lap. Steadying me with one strong hand, he rubbed his dick back and forth between my wet folds, and then guided the head into the heated abyss.

He felt glorious! I do not think that I have been stretched out or filled as much as this before and I liked it. Wrapping his hand inside my hair again, he began to lay the pipe faster. Building the rhythm, we fell into sync while I am riding his dick. Thwack! He slaps my ass so hard, it sounds out. It was painful, but dear God, it felt so good.

"Oh my God!" I could hold back any longer, the harder he pushed the harder I met every single thrust. "I... am... going... to ...cum!" With a high-pitched squeal, I burst into a million pieces. Jerome was not done with my ass yet. He bent me over my table and started hitting it from the back. Thwack, thwack, thwack! A hand slipped around my throat pulling me, so he can go deeper.

He growled and I felt him grow even more within me. Growls thwack! "Emma! Baby put that ass in the air for me!" he growls. Thwack! "Oh my god Emma! I'm about to cum!" With another growl, he came all inside of me. I should not have let him do that, but I really did not care at this point. He pulled me over to the chair and watched me, when he saw the redness and welts on my side and ass; he kept repeating how sorry he was and did not mean to be so rough with me. I laughed.

"So, how about inviting me over now to talk about the case?" he looked at me intensely for about what felt like five minutes. Then, we broke out into laughter.

"Ok I'll invite you this one time, but only if you'll buy some Chinese food and wine to go with those files," he contemplated this, but from the look he gave me, I knew the case will not be in the future for the rest of the night.

Ok okay, you think I am crazy. Really, it is not as bad as it seems. I got my back blown out by a complete total stranger. Well technically, I knew him since high school.

Ask me if I care? Go on ask me?! Nope! I said to myself laughing.

Looking over my shoulder at Jerome, who sat in my passenger seat looking all content with himself, I was ecstatic for once. My body was sedated and my mind was at ease. Now, I have a dirty little secret, but I do not think I would be able to watch my boss in his face without blushing. I was fucking his son and it felt sooooooo good and I could not help but sing to myself! You go girl! Nevertheless, let the record state, I did NOT start this!

Chapter 2

I was hooked! I called his hotel every day for about a week so I could get the dick. When he did not answer, I showed up unannounced. If it annoyed him, well I was sure as hell oblivious to that fact. Then he disappeared and I was out in the cold once again.

About 3 weeks later, I was pregnant and miserable. Jerome still was nowhere to be found. What should I do? Do I walk up to his dad and demand to know where he is? Nope, if he thinks that he is going to leave me in this condition, he had another thing coming.

****

SEVEN MONTHS LATER....

It has now been about seven months since I last seen Jerome and as you have guessed, I am huge. *Regales and Ports* is the one place I do not want to be at this point. All the side-glances and the whispers behind my back, it's downing and with my hormones, I was snapping and cussing everyone out.

As I swaddled to the bathroom for the umpteenth time today, I heard my coworker, Michelle, laughing with someone on the phone telling them I did not know who my baby's father was. I was livid! Just as I was going to turn into her office to confront her, tall, dark and scrumptious walked into the front door. As much as I planned revenge, I was not quite up to the task yet.

I took one good look at him and all thoughts of evil vanished. Nope! I needed to hide fast. Where? How the hell would I know, I just needed to get back to my office before he spotted me. I turned in the direction of my office and walked as quickly as my feet could take me.

Safely tucked away in my corner from everybody, I tried to relax. Man, I need to pee! Old man McKinney has not been in for about a week now and the clients were getting restless. Just as I was getting comfortable and settling into my chair,

Michelle, my co-worker, walked into my office stating that Junior had an announcement.

While everyone crowded into the reception area, I snuck off to the bathroom to relieve myself. Yes! Scored one for Emma! I stayed close to the back, hoping he would not see me. My, how the mighty has fallen. From small time earning, her way to top lawyer to major scaredy cat, hiding as far as possible in the back as I can.

I tried to blend into the crowd of my coworkers but it was to no avail. Jerome spotted me, very pregnant, and I hung my head in shame as he began to speak.

"In the sudden light of my father's death, I will be taking over and making some drastic changes around here," Audible collective gasps sounded out around the room. "Look to your left. Look to your right. Your friend and coworker might not be here tomorrow." My heart sunk.

"Sir, this is exactly what this office needs. Welcome aboard!" Michelle's annoying voice floated through the crowd. As I looked up, she was standing right in front of him trying to get his attention, by touching his arm and flirting heavily with him, yet his gaze was on me. Whelp!

"Many of you seem to look at me with worried looks on your faces and you should be. We will be downsizing the company over the next three to four years. Any dishonest or deceitful behaviors will be found and dealt with. I will have my personal auditor look over our budgets and files and I will await his report. That would be all for today."

Everyone started murmuring at once and right now, I want to die! Thinking to myself, I asked, "Emma, how do you find yourself in these messes?" Replying "Jeez self, I really don't know!"

Now, how am I going to explain to Jerome that I am pregnant with his baby? Okay, can we please take this one day at a time? I am going to tell him, well sort of, but not right now.

Moving closer and closer to the exit, I panicked when Jerrod, the maintenance man, tapped me on the shoulder. Smiling sweetly, I asked him what was the problem and he had the nerve to ask me about what Jerome said! Did he realize I am trying to save my life here?

Well, so much for a clean escape. Jerome was barreling towards me and I could actually see the steam radiating off his ears.

"You, my office, NOW!" At this point, everyone's attention was on me. Jerome pivoted on his heels and headed towards what used to be his dad's office. I dragged my feet, as I felt like I was walking to my doom. I was still looking for an escape, if not, I was just going to make his life a living hell.

"Today, Ms. Ross, today!" I sighed, because that was not what he was calling me the last time I saw him. His authority turned me on, but this was not the time and place for my hormones to be in their feelings. He stood in the doorway tapping his foot, and then slammed the door closed as soon as I was inside.

"I was coming sir. Obviously, you can't see that I am pregnant," I said through clenched teeth. I felt like I could hear everyone's thoughts outside the door.

"Does anyone know what she did?"

"Is she the first to go?"

"Is he the baby's father?" Everyone was talking at once. I felt like they were outside the door playing jeopardy on the reason why I was in the boss' office.

"So what's new, Emma? How you been? WOW really a baby? You don't say," Jerome was pissed; I could feel it permeating off him, as he rattled off questions one behind the other. "Well are you going to say anything for yourself, Emma?"

"Umm, Hi? And where the fuck have you been?"

"Damn it, Emma! You mean to tell me after what we went through you went out and got pregnant!" he completely ignored my question.

"You ignored my question Jerome," a silent weight lifted off my shoulders, but it was quickly replaced by anger that was slowly climbing up my chest. "And wait what we had? Really?! What the fuck did we have?!" By now, my voice was screeching to the top of my lungs and I am pretty sure that everyone outside of the room could have heard me. "You're the one that disappeared without a fucking trace!"

Jerome rounded the table and was on his knees in front of me trying to calm me down.

"Hey, hey shhh shhh, I'm sorry. I am sorry. Just tone your voice down some. That was wrong of me. I am happy that you found someone and you are starting a family. I'm just a little jealous, that all." The tears were falling now. My hormones are really malfunctioning today.

"Get off of me!" I seethe. "Dude, are you fucking ignorant or are you that blind to the obvious Jerome?" he paused.

"What do you mean?" I could feel the tension building back into the room.

"Oh my god, for fuck sakes, Jerome the baby is yours." My heart stopped for a split second and I swore I seen the bones in his face flex with angry. Without another word, Jerome strolled through the door and out of the building with a bang, leaving me to the judgment of my coworkers.

Was I crushed? Yes, and no, but I expected it. What else could I have done at that point in time, but tell him the truth? I thought about telling him that the baby was not his, but that would be unfair to both him and the baby, so I took the better course of action.

Heading back to my office, I felt like holes were being burned into my back. Planting my ass firmly within my seat, I looked at the Mackenzie Trial in front of me. This was the reason I decided to tell Jerome because I did not want to be like her. Lorna Mackenzie, who was on the verge of losing her three-year-old son to billionaire Ted Wakes.

Her mistake you ask? She did not tell the wealthy oil tycoon that she was sleeping with, that she had his child. Now, he is out for blood and wants her to pay for time lost. He is also fighting for full custody of his heir.

Sad right? Yes, I know, but I refuse to be her and I will do anything to make sure my baby was okay. Just then, Michelle walked into my office looking all-dapper, as if she just won the lottery.

"Soooooo, You and the new boss seem to be hitting it off just fine." Can I punch her in the face please? I really want to.

"Can you get the hell out of my office? Please and thank you." I am counting to ten, so I do not get fired today. 1...2...3...4...5

"Ok I'll bite, I'm just curious, why is Jerome McKinney Jr. so pissed at you?" 10...9...8...7....6

"Personally, that is none of your God damn business.

"Well, it did seem so to everyone on the outside. All we were hearing is GONE….BABY…. PISSED, then he storms out. Did he fire you because of the baby?"

"Wouldn't you just love that?" I gave a sickly sweet smile.

"One can only wish," her grin spread from ear to ear. Just as I was about to give her a piece of my mind, Jerome's towering frame appeared and I almost could kiss him. Talk about saved by the bell!

"Can you excuse us, Ms. Tarver?"

I never saw Michelle so frightened in my life. She took the color scarlet to a whole different level. "Sure, of course, Mr. McKinney," And with that, she was out of my hair.

"Let's go," The statement was not one to be ignored, but I pushed his buttons anyway.

"I am not going anywhere, especially with you. I am in the middle of the workday, I have things to do. Plus, everyone is already watching my every move since our little extravagant encounter."

"Do not argue with me Emma, I guarantee you will not win and will regret it," The look in his eyes told me not to fight anymore, but I did not care.

"I am not going! Are you deaf?" Quickly, he grabs me by my shoulder and pulled me towards the door. I pulled away, reached for my bag under the desk and followed behind him, without a word.

As we were passing the reception area, he told Marcy to hold all his calls and that I would be out for the rest of the week. I turned to argue, but the look he shot me, snapped my mouth shut. Sigh, if that look could have kill, I would be six feet under by now.

Jerome guided me towards the front of the building, then to where his car was parked. To tell you the truth, I was scared. I have seen episodes of *SNAPPED and* I not trying to be one of those victims.

"Where are we going?"

"Get in," Again with the ordering, but because I did not feel like arguing with him, I got in.

****

Driving on I-95 North, we sat in silence. I did not know what to say to him. He was a one-weekend stand. Seriously, how did my life get like this? I was wallowing in self-pity when he finally spoke.

"Were you ever going to tell me?" it was genuine question, so instead of picking a fight, I tried to sound like the mature civilized adult I am supposed to be.

"To tell you the truth, no I wasn't," I heard him take a sharp breath, so I continued explaining. "I had no contact from you in seven months, Jerome. What was I really supposed to tell you?" The car went quiet again.

"I'm sorry," I heard him mumble the phrase, but I was not too sure on what I heard. "I'm sorry," he repeated again when I looked at him as if he lost his damn mind. "I didn't even think on that aspect of the situation and it's not like you would have asked my dad to contact me about the situation," he rushed on to say.

"My baby is not a situation," I looked at him narrowing my eyes.

"Yes, of course. I apologize. Wrong choice of words," I relaxed a bit. "So, when are you due, Emma?"

"Well, we are in March and I made seven months officially today, so three months from now would be June. June 26th."

"The day after my mom's birthday, this will be a great surprise for her. She's always asking me when I am going to get married to give her some grandkids," he looked at me and smiled. I could not stay mad at him anymore, and it is exhausting.

Just then, he pulled into a lake front property that was tucked away behind the trees. I had a million and one questions and was looking and planning an escape route in my head, just in case, he tried to kill me out here.

Walking into the house, there was a small group of people hustling through the house. "What's this?" "What?" he countered. "Don't look at me like that. I have no clue what is going on, as usual," I sincerely said.

"Well, I can't have the mother of my child all stressed out. When I left the office today, I passed a spa, so I went in to ask couple of questions and now, we are here."

"You got me this way," I said under my breath. Damn, there go those hormones again. The tears began to fall again and I could not help but think that I found that most perfectly unperfected man in the world, who just happened to be my boss.

Is this type of treatment going to continue? Gee, I really do not know. Am I going to enjoy it? Hell to the yes!

All my life I dreamed of a fairy tale to come true and now that it kind of has, I am going to hold it by the horns and never let it go.

Chapter 3

So, where do I begin? I am in love! Finally. Yes, I said finally! I know most people think that it is not something that you can do just like that, but I am.

Jerome and I are as night and day, especially being that we live in two different states, but do we really care? Well, I do not and Jerome does not seem to be making any noise about it.

The months are moving by quickly and we have been hustling to get the nursery together at my house. Standing by the window of the living room, I am waiting for Jerome to bring the car seat to me from *Baby's R Us*. Our little girl was sure to be spoiled! A familiar hum of a car approaching made the butterflies start fluttering again.

Somehow, I can never get used to it. As fast as I could, I waddled towards the door in the kitchen, but when I opened it, it was not who I was expecting. To make things even more awkward, Jerome pulled in just behind them. Shit! No, no, no, they are not supposed to be here! "Mom? Dad? How are you?" I tried my best to get excited to see them, but I could tell this was not going to be the exciting visit that you would expect. Dear God, why me?

"Sweetheart? How are you?" The confusion on her face, needless to say, was priceless and my dad, on the other hand, has not said anything up to now. Mr. Joseph Ross just stood there like a large granite statue and inspected me from head to toe. I need to get out of here, like fast!

I know everyone is going to be all like that is your family, they came to help out, do not be frightened. Blah, blah, blah. One mucho grandè problemo, I did not tell them I was pregnant.

I know it was stupid, but in my defense, it completely slipped my mind! Ok, that was a lie. My parents and I are not exactly on great terms. I do not call them and they surely do not call me. I really did not care. I got the peace I was looking for and there was no one to judge me on my life decisions.

The last time I spoke to them was the day I left for college to become a lawyer. My dad was mad and been has mad at me ever since, because he wanted me to take over the family business of selling cars.

"Come in, come in. I guess we have a lot to talk about today. When did you guys get into town?" As I ushered them into the living room, Jerome gave me the, "What the fuck is going on" look. Shaking my head, I pulled him close to me, as I know I am going to need him. As I look around my domain, I noticed Jerome was moving slowly, it is funny that I never noticed it before.

"So Emma, when were you going to tell us you were pregnant?" cutting right to the situation at hand, my dad wasted no time.

"Joseph! Stop it!" my mom turned a bright crimson red on her caramel honey toned skin. Oh no, here we go….

"What Maryanne?! Emma needs to answer the damned question!"

"Now, wait a minute dad, I'm not a kid!" Oh My God! This is so embarrassing!

"No, you're not a kid but you're my kid!"

"Daaadddddd! Stop it! Now, you want to treat me like I am your kid?" I felt the tears welling up behind my eyelids. Damn these hormones. I pulled myself together.

I could see Jerome standing by the couch watching in disbelief, not sure, if he should say anything. At this point, I felt helpless. This was my "Picture Perfect" moment, but I forgot how my family could get when brought into the picture. "You know what, dad, I'm sorry. I know you had high hopes for your business and me. I am sorry but I wanted to be a lawyer. You feel like I have let you down, but you are not going to waltz into my life and turn it upside down, after not even answering or returning any calls after six fucking years!" Hanging my head, I started walking out of the room and for the first time since my parents stormed into town, I heard Jerome speak.

"Baby no, do not do that," Jerome pulled me close to him, hugging and kissing the top of my head. I swore I saw steam coming out my dad's ears as he witnessed the tender moment that just passed between Jerome and I. I, Emma Ross, his child could actually be happy!

"Emma, who is this?" I was breathing slowly yet, he still have not responded to anything I said before.

"Dad, this is Jerome," Breathe Emma breathe. "He is my boyfriend and the baby's father."

"Maryanne, let's go," And with that, my parents left my house.

Jerome turned to me, inspecting me, "Emma, what the hell was that about?" I wish I could have really explained to him what just happened.

"Honey, that… that was my family."

"Well Emma, I got that part, but the reaction to you being pregnant and well, me being the father, is what I don't get."

"I didn't tell them."

"Emma!"

"I know, I know, I fucked up, I'm sorry! As I said, I have not spoken to them in six years. I don't even know why they were just here!"

"My God, Em, we are inviting them back over tomorrow and you're going to sit and talk to them, while I am at work," no the hell he did not! I swear, if I did not love him.

"What?! Do I really have to?"

"Yes, you do," towering over me, he rained kisses from the top of my head down my neck. Oh my! "Right now, I want you from the back, I feel kind of naughty."

How could I deny him? His skilled fingers were already making tracks up and down my legs. The robe I had on was no match for Mr. McKinney Jr. Guiding me towards the arm of the couch; he bent me over and dropped my panties to the floor. Slipping his finger into my hot core, his name hissed out of my mouth. Again, he repeated the gesture with an extra finger. As you have noticed, it does not take much for to get me excited. "Baby I need you," he whispered again.

"Well, take me then," I challenged. Jerome did not have to be told twice. Still playing with my womanhood, he juggled pleasuring my clit and unzipping his pants. I felt him remove his hand and slid inside of me.

****

Monday was a hectic one. I gained two more cases to my ever-growing pile. Looking through the latest case, Michelle walked into the door grinning like a damn Cheshire cat. Boy, what I wouldn't give to wipe that smirk off her face."

"You're   back!" one…two…three…four…five…

"Yes, I'm back. I was only gone on a weeklong vacation, Michelle. What do you need?" I closed the file.

"Ooooo, bitchy are we?" I rolled my eyes and repeated the question. "Ok okay, the office been buzzing since you left, you know." Ok, I will bite on this one.

"Really? About what?" Although the suspense was killing me to find out, I declined to indulge in it. "Wait! Don't tell me, I don't care."

"Well, everyone thought that you were fired last week," Michelle chuckled.

"I assure you, I am still right here."

"So I see. But moving on too juicier details, who is the mysterious baby daddy Ems that is what I want to know." Ten...nine.... eight.... seven...six

"Why is that your fucking business Michelle? Trust, I am not sleeping with your man. Oh that's right, you don't have one!" Slowly, I smiled. A movement by the door of my cubicle caught my eye. There was Jerome, looking amused at the turn of the conversation, as he walked in the door. I was grateful.

"Michelle! How are you doing? Have you finished with the Siegfried case yet? I would love to go over it today, before I go to the MCM Conference in Atlanta." Atlanta? Wait, why I did not know about this?

By this time, Michelle was beat red with embarrassment and edged towards the door, "I'll go finish that for you right away." With that, she was gone. Relief flooded me, but another motion soon began to creep in.

"Atlanta huh? When were you going to tell me?" I was a little taken back by his revelation, but I was pissed.

"Awe Ems, please don't be mad, I just got the call this morning. Now, I'm in here with you," I hate him.

"Ok fine, I won't be mad this time, but you're sleeping on the couch tonight," I gave him a little pout and turned back to the pile on my desk. Swiftly, he dropped to his knees and kissed my forehead.

"I will do no such thing," and he was out the door before anyone noticed.

The rest of the day past by in a blur and I could not wait to head home. For some reason, Jerome has been on my mind since this morning. Driving into the supermarket parking lot, my phone rang. Guess who? Smiling, I answered.

"What are you wearing?" the deep rumble in his voice washed over me.

"The same thing I had on this morning and I look like a fucking fat cow, why?" I laughed as I walked into the fresh produce aisle.

"Hmm, what a fresh kill you will be when I get you in my bed," his voice got deeper.

"Oh My God! No, you did not just agree that I look like a cow!"

"No baby, I was only agreeing on how beautiful you looked this morning. I can't wait to cater to you after your parents leave, once dinner is over."

"Shit, shit, shit, shit, shit!"

"Emma, you forgot, didn't you?!"

"Jerome, I'm sorry I did! Shit, I really do not want to go through this again. You know what, I will hang up with you and call my mom right away."

Hanging up from him, I took a deep breath before I rang my mother's phone. As the phone rang, I prayed she did not answer, but my prayers went unheard.

"Emma, is that you? How are you feeling honey?" I paused for a moment, thinking on what to say to her. As I start to speak, the words would not form. "Emma, are you there?"

"Yes, I'm here. I'm doing great mom, how are you and dad?"

"I'm fine sweetie and so is your father. You know he is still mad at you.

"How can he be mad? Mom, you know we do not speak. I'm sorry mom, things just happened."

"Well you know your father. He will be just fine, just give it a couple days. He keeps ranting about "the hoodlum" that knocked you up!" I could not help but start laughing because I could almost hear my dad muttering to himself, as he takes a beer from the fridge.

"Mom Jerome is far from a hoodlum, you know. He is actually a very successful lawyer."

"I know dear, I know. Well, your father wants us to go to the bar next door; I'll talk to you later."

"Mom! Wait, before you go, would you and dad like to come over for dinner tomorrow night?"

"That would be great honey. I will discuss it with your father and call you before the night is out."

"Thanks mom. Talk to you soon."

Finally, after the conversation I had with my mom, I got out the car and walked into the store. Tonight is looking like a Caesar Salad type of night. As I gathered the things to make the salad, I noticed a tall woman at the counter just staring at me. Why was this bitch watching me like that? Smiling politely, I made my way to the cashier to pay for my goods when I heard her speak.

"Excuse me, ma'am?"

"Yes?" I tried not to be rude, but I really did not understand why she was bugging me. I just want to go home to my man.

"Sorry, I didn't mean to disturb you; I just wanted to say congratulations on your pregnancy. How far along are you?"

Smiling again to be polite, I answered as I handed the cashier the money for the items I purchased, "I am eight and a half months pregnant and I can't wait to meet her!" I hope the fake excitement was not too much.

"That is beautiful! Well, I must be running now, you take care. Congratulations again!" Okay, that was weird. It was time to get home, I said to myself, as I rolled my eyes.

****

As I pulled up to the door, I noticed Jerome was already inside, washing the left over dishes from yesterday.

"Baby, I'm home," I called as I entered into the kitchen.

"Awesome, I'm starved!" he said as he kissed me. "Where are your parents?"

"They are coming tomorrow baby, promise."

"Is everything alright with them?" I could tell he had a bit of concern on his face, but I smiled to reassure him.

"Yes Jerome, everything will be fine, don't worry about it too much. Mom has everything under control, trust me."

As our night moved forward, I could not help but think on what happened in the store today. The look in her eyes was of pure sadness, as if she could not conceive her own. I know I may sound crazy, but I have a sneaky feeling it would not be the last time I saw her.

Chapter 4

Ok, I am scared, and I do not mean needle prick type of scared. Lately, Jerome has been out of town going to conferences in Atlanta and Miami. I am now in my last week of pregnancy and life is about to change. At this point, I really have started doubting myself. Will I be a great mother? Will I teach her the right things? I really do not know. All I know is that I want Jerome at home with me and it was getting on my nerves that he was never here.

Today, I called his phone like a million times. He did not answer a phone call, nor did he call to say he was busy or dying. I was growing tired of this. As I walked to the car to go to work, a sharp pain shot up from the base of my spine. After ten seconds, it stopped. Well, that was harsh! Lately, I had been having some pain, but I did not think anything of it.

Pulling into the parking lot of *Regales and Ports*, another pain gripped me as I walked into the building. I seriously need to sit my ass down. Today, I feel as if I am on death row. Everyone just stared at me as I took a seat in my cubicle. As if on cue, Michelle came into my office and just looked at me as I stared at the pile of papers on my desk, willing it to go away. In the far distance, I heard my name, but at this point, I was not too sure of what I was hearing as another pain crippled me. I screamed.

"Emma! Emma! Are you ok?" I thought I actually saw genuine concern on Michelle's face, for once.

"Michelle......call 911," I panted. I was so tired, I just wanted to sleep, but there was too much pain at once. If I knew what I know now, there would not be a baby. I do not know how other women do this.

"Emma, breathe and take deep breaths. The ambulance is on its way," as another crippling pain took over me, I noticed a crowd starting to form outside of my cubicle.

Within twenty minutes, the ambulance had arrived and I was strapped to their bed in five minutes. As they carried me on our one-way ticket to the hospital, there he was, standing on the side panic-stricken. Weaving through the crowd, he made his way towards the ambulance and started to get in.

"Sir, you cannot get in here," I heard the paramedic tell Jerome. I wish they would keep it down, not everyone need to hear this. I was mad and furious at him. The truth was I did not want him anywhere close to me.

"Jerome, please don't cause a goddamn scene!" He ignored my request and continued to rant at the paramedic.

"The hell I can't! Are you going to fucking stop me? Huh? If you do not let me onto this ambulance, I will sue the pants right off your scrawny ass!"

"Sir, do what you please, but if you are not related to her, I can't let you on here. Even if you're her boss!" the paramedic had guts, I could tell you.

"Jerome, just stop!" Another pain hit me and they were wasting precious time arguing. I mean, I could have stopped it by just saying he was the father, but I did not want to announce it to the crowd.

"I'm the fucking father, you nitwit!" The paramedic paled and a collection of gasps sounded off, right outside of the vehicle. I groaned. I had to be invisible and my words not heard. Well, there goes my job. I cannot work here anymore; my reputation I tried so hard to keep is now ruined!

"Jerome, stop it and sit next to me, please. Everyone can hear you." Although my voice was soft, he heard me and complied, but kept apologizing for not being home this weekend.

"I'm sorry, I should have been here! You would have never come to work this morning. I don't care if the office has something to say, I own the place!" I chuckled a little bit. In addition, I thought I was the drama queen!

"It's ok, let's just go have this baby," I gave a short smile and with that, they shut the doors and we were off.

****

Inside the hospital, the doctors worked quickly. They hooked me up to IVs, took vitals and the whole nine yards. As I lay in the bed, I remembered that I have to call my parents to let them know they are about to be grandparents. I pictured my dad, holding my little girl as I closed my eyes. Although, we do not get along, there was nothing like having them here to see their grandchild. Maybe I have been delusional for a while because it almost sounds like I hear them now!

I slowly open my eyes to find my mother standing over me, rubbing a cool cloth on my forehead.

"Oh baby, my poor baby, you're finally awake!" Mother was always dramatic, but I was glad she was here.

"Mom, how did you know I was here?"

"Don't be silly, honey. Jerome called and told us you were on the way to the hospital. I came as soon as possible. Your father will be here in an hour or two; he had to finish working his shift."

Cannot say that I was not a little disappointed, but at least he was coming, that was a good thing. Just then, my doctor came and started prodding and poking me, making sure the baby and I were all right. Just as he was about to leave the room, he estimated that I would be about another half an hour, if that much.

Ok, I need these damn pains to stop! About fifteen minutes later, my contractions were less than two minutes apart and a flurry of nurses rushed Jerome and I into the delivery room. Looking over at him, I saw the fear in his eyes. Rubbing his hand was all I could do to comfort him.

****

After last night's events, things had quieted down and all I could do was stare at her. She was perfect. This was really it! I was a mom and I could only hope that I would be as great as my mom was to me. It was late, about 10:15 pm, when my dad knocked on the door. Watching the bundle in my hands, I finally saw his face lighting up, reminding me of the man he once was. Slowly, he edged towards the bed.

"Is that her? Is that my grandbaby?" Smiling, I handed him my small joy.

"Yes, daddy. This is your granddaughter, Isobel Marie McKinney." His eyes shone when he realized that I named her after his mother. I mean, really it is the least that I can do. No, that is not the truth. It is the only name I could think of at that point.

"Hi Isobel, this is your grandpa," Isobel snuggled deeper into him and I smiled. The last thing I remembered, before I drifted off to sleep, is my dad cooing over the baby, calling her Izzy.

All night, Jerome just hovered at the door, scared to come in. He was in the delivery room, but passed out when Izzy was crowning. I waved for him to come in, but he hesitated. If my legs were not still so weak…

Slowly, he entered the room, trying to be careful not to wake my dad and the sleeping baby.

"Hi," he whispered, as he sat down next to me on the bed.

"Hi. I'm still mad at you," searching his face, I tried to figure out what was up with him, but decided to leave well enough alone.

"I know. How are you?"

If you were here, you would have known how I was! I smiled.

"I'm alright. Doctor said that I should be out of here by tomorrow, so I am about to get some rest before we get home," I smiled again.

Looking at his face, I noticed he still seemed a tad distant and tired, but I was tired myself. Since it seemed like he did not have anything else to say, I rolled over onto my side and swiftly fell into one of my mini comas in La La Land. Sometimes during the night, my dad left the room and even without me being awake, I could tell the difference instantly.

I slowly slipped out my coma to find Jerome pacing the floor with Izzy making gargling noises and baby talk to help. He definitely looked ten times better than before I went to sleep. As I laid there, an overwhelmed feeling of something was not right too over me and at this point, I did not care what the consequences were.

"Hey," he looked up at me and smiled. My stomach did summersaults.

"Hey. Emma, thank you. My baby girl, OUR baby girl is beautiful," I felt somewhat guilty at this point, but I blurted out what I was feeling anyway.

"Jerome, baby I need to know what is going on between us. You have been away A LOT lately. I know you're now the owner of your father's company, but honey it's starting to get weird." As the shock dissipated from his face, he slowly placed Izzy back into her little plastic crib and sat next to me.

"Emma, what are you trying to tell me right now? Are you telling me you want to break up?" Can

I smack him pleasssseee? I sat there looking at him as if he had three heads.

"Did you hear anything I just said? I never said I want to leave you, but I would like to know what is going on with you lately."

"I'm sorry baby, I really am. I do not mean to seem like I am axing you out. I just been having so much going on lately with the office and I didn't feel like stressing you out, while you were pregnant." I searched his face to see if I could find an inclination that he was lying, but could get that vibe. His phone rang.

"Ok baby, fair enough, but when you're going through it remember, I go through it also. I am here for you!" I swore I saw the tears welled up in his eyes, or so I thought. I know things have been a little hard, but I did not expect to see the scene in front of me happening. He turned and left to answer the phone.

****

Today was a new day! After my very short conversation with Jerome last night, I was on my way home with Izzy and my man by my side. Just before we got to the house, we decided to stop in at a local *Texas Roadhouse*, so that we can get a good meal, then head to bed.

Once inside of the restaurant, I glimpsed at a few familiar faces, but one stood out to me the most. I smiled at her, but kept it moving heading in the direction that Jerome disappeared in. When I got to my table, I noticed that Jerome was not there and the woman that I smiled at earlier came over.

"Is this the lovely baby?" she squealed. This bitch is crazy! I swore she fell in love with Izzy on site.

"Hi, yes...yes it is, her name is Isobel." Why I just told her that I do not know, but for some reason, I felt comfortable around this woman. "I'm sorry, what did you say your name was again?"

"Oh, pardon me! My name is Maria D'Souza McKinney, but everyone calls me Suzie!" I swear the woman's pepped up personality sickens me. That last name is quiet familiar. I wonder if she and Jerome are family members. I will have to ask later, if I remember.

"Well Mrs. McKinney, it was nice to meet you, but I am about to use the bathroom really quick before my boyfriend comes back." With that, I got up from the table and walked away.

For some reason, this woman had been showing up and although, I felt comfortable around her, something was not right. Being the yellow belly chicken that I am, I do not think I am trying to find out who she really is or what she really wants. Little did I know, Jerome stood in the doorway watching the whole encounter, while on his phone and I was oblivious to the whole situation.

About a half an hour later, Izzy was safely nestled in her crib in the corner of the room and Jerome and I were cuddled on the bed.

"Baby?" I felt him stirring behind of me.

"Yeah?"

"Do you know a Maria D'Souza McKinney?" I swore I felt him stiffen behind me, but it was such a felting moment, I almost missed it.

"No, why baby?" I hesitated for a moment before I replied. I felt he was lying, but I do not want to get into it just yet, without some facts.

"Nothing really, honey. Do not worry about it. It is just a woman I have been running into a lot lately and today, she finally introduced herself at the roadhouse. I just wondered if you knew her."

"Oh ok, well baby, the name don't ring a bell. Maybe it's one of the girl's dad used to mess around with on mom. Not too sure and right now, this is where I am, here is where I would love to be, for the rest of my life, with you." I felt the tingle of his words flowing over my skin and with that, he pulled me in closer to him. I fell asleep thinking, *but she has your last name.*

Chapter 5

Oh my God! This is all I could think to myself as I looked over my calendar. Isobel is now about four months old and it was time for me to head back to work. After Jerome's big admission in front of everyone at work, I am not too sure, how comfortable things will be for me there now, but starting Monday morning bright and early, I will be there.

As I walked to the living room, I heard the doorbell ring. I wonder who it can be at this hour. Opening the door, Izzy started to cry. A young woman, about thirty years old, flew into my house towards the baby's bedroom.

"Miss! Miss! Who the hell are you?" I was pissed. I could not believe that this woman really just walked into my house and straight into my baby's room.

"The baby miss, she is crying!" Wait, who the hell is this woman and how the fuck she knows that, she is a she? There I am standing here, I am sure looking like a buffoon, watching this woman pick up my child and try to soothe her.

"Ok lady, I am going to ask you one last time, who the fuck are you? You gotten seconds before I rip a new fucking ass hole in you," bouncing the baby in her arms, she finally looked at me and answered.

"I am Rhoda, Ms. Ross!" she was scared, but still answered a little too cheery for my linking. I am sulking now. "Yes, Mr. McKinney Jr. sent me. To help with the baby," I continued to stare off into space. "Ms. Ross? You ok?" I looked her squared in the eyes and smiled.

"Yes, I'm fine," With that, I turned out of Izzy's bedroom and walked into mine.

While in the bedroom, I began fuming. I mean like really, how could he make this decision without me! I swear every time I go to pick up the phone, the choice words that comes to mind to tell him, would make your ears bleed.

At the same time I actually dialed the number, Jerome walked in the door, shouting my name. As I walked out of the bedroom, I was mentally throwing daggers at his ass, as he walked into the kitchen.

Standing in the doorway, he came up to me with this smug smile on his face and kissed me on the forehead. Oh My God, I could kill him now! "How was your day baby?" *How was your day baby?*

"Who the fuck do you really think you are? Oh let us see, Jerome shall we, hmm how was my day? I was in the mist of prepping for work on Monday and here comes Super Rhoda, storming into my fucking house! Straight to my child claiming you sent her and that she is the nanny! A fucking nanny really? Get her the fuck out of here now!"

"Whoa, hold on, so you're upset about the nanny?" Jerome stood there like a lost little schoolboy.

"Yes! I am upset! Not the fact that you wanted to give me help. Nooooooo! One, you did it behind my mother fucking back without discussing it with me first. Two, you didn't even have the balls to tell me that she was coming!" Looking at him, I saw that I struck a nerve, but did I care? NOPE!

"Emma are you really serious right now? Since when do I justify everything that I do to you?" No, the fuck, he did not!

"The fuck you mean by that Jerome? The last I checked, you did not bring that child into the world on your own. You didn't carry her for fucking nine months? You had my help also! Being a good parent takes team work, not me work!" Slowly, he backed away from me. I swear with the looks that were passing back and forth between the both of us, it was about to be World War III up in this bitch.

"Woman, you done lost your mother fucking mind! Why is this even an issue? You need the help and you go back to work on Monday, why are you being a bitch about this?" Ouch!

"A bitch huh?"

"Emma, no, don't take that the wrong way!"

With that, he reached for my hand, but I pulled away. "We will be at my parents' house. When I get back, I want you out my damn house." My voice was frozen over. I had enough.

****

Sitting at my mom's table, I felt like a teenager again, waiting for my dad to come home because I was in deep trouble. Daddy, for some reason, always knew how to make it better. Maybe, I was wrong. I highly doubt that. Maybe, just maybe, I overreacted. Umm nope, did not think that either. I just do not know what possessed him to do something like that.

Within ten minutes of me being there, daddy walked through the door from work. He looked so old and weary now. Maybe, this was a bad idea coming. Just as I was about to leave the kitchen to hide in the living room for a couple minutes, daddy stopped me in the hallway.

"So, to what do your mother and I owe this pleasure of seeing you?" I swear, I felt like the smallest piece of garbage trampled under his stare.

"Nothing daddy, Jerome and I had an argument and I didn't feel like staying at home."

"Come with me in the kitchen child." I hate when he does that. I am not a baby anymore, dad! Well I ran home to my parents like a little kid, so I guess I had that one coming. "What is going on with you two? I thought you all was so in love!" Out of the corner of my eye, I saw my mom peek in and disappear again.

"Umm well today, some random woman showed up on my door step," I twiddled my fingers. "When I opened the door, Izzy started crying and she rushed in and went straight to her room, and picked your up." I twiddled some more.

"If you don't stop fidgeting with your damn hands girl!" I felt like shit again.

"Sorry. Now dad, I do not like that. Apparently, Jerome hired this woman to take care of Izzy when I go back to work, without my knowledge."

"Why would the fuck he do something like that?" I saw the actually concern and aggravation in his eyes.

"I don't know and what pissed me off the most, he made it sound like he was the one that carried that child for nine months. Dad, he only came back into the picture when I was seven months pregnant."

My dad sighed as if he had a heavy heart. "This is not what I wanted for you, but I am not going to lecture you about it. You are a grown woman. What I am about to tell you, I do hope that you do not get upset with me." My stomach fell.

"Ok daddy."

"While you were sleeping at the hospital, I had a chance to speak to Jerome and frankly baby, I don't like him. Too arrogant for my taste, but there is something still about him. Ems, something just does not feel right. He spent a lot of the time on the phone talking about some kind of account and large figures. I didn't hear much, but it seems fishy"

As I sat there listening to my father's confession, I did not even know how to reply at this point. I sat and thought on the pass year with my current boyfriend. I could not tell whether we were coming or going within the relationship. He was always gone and I needed to find out why.

I tried to make sure everything was fine up until the stunt he pulled today, and now it makes me wonder, if maybe I have been blinded by love all this time. My dad looked at me and sensed that I knew exactly what he was talking about. "Well, I guess baby girl, you have a lot to think about. I am going to take a shower and take your mother to bed."

"Ok daddy." My voice was barely audible.

****

Oh my God! I cannot believe it is my first day back at work, already! Walking through the doors of *Regal and Ports*, I felt a renewed energy and pep in my step, as I got to my desk, but it was soon short lived.

Rounding the corner, there was Jerome, next to Michelle's desk, going over the latest on something they were working on. Her flirting and touching was at an all-time high and watching them, I felt sick and disgusted. Just as I went to open the door, she looked up, pointed to him trying not to look so inconspicuous, throwing the thumbs up sign at me. Oh boy, it is going to be a lonnnng day. The bitch knew just how to irk the hell out of me!

Pulling myself back to reality, I waved back at her, just to keep the peace hoping and praying to God that no one will come and interrogate me on Jerome. Most of all, I prayed to God that Jerome does not hassle me in my office.

The day flew by quickly. Thank God! As I packed up my things to leave the office and pick up

Izzy from my parents' house, I realized it was as if everyone was working overtime today. Just as I picked up my purse from under my desk, Jerome shouted for me to come into his office. Crap!

"Come in and close the door," his voice was steeled with authority and insolence, but I just played as if I did not notice it. "Are you coming home tonight?" he asked, soon as I shut the door.

"No, I am not. I am staying with my mother until you get rid of that woman you brought into my house! And I thought I told you, I want you gone?" I mean I was a little too loud, but I really did not care.

"No darling, my house and I am not getting rid of the nanny that I brought in to help you!" Crap that hurt! His house? He forgot that I bought that house before him? Humph!

"Your house?! YOUR HOUSE?! Really Jerome? Where the fuck was you when I signed the mother fucking deed to the place? That's right, nowhere!" My voice was on high now.

"Do not address me by my first name while we are in this office!" My eyes widened at that.

"The fuck you mean, Je-rome," I said, enunciating every syllable. "The fuck is wrong with you? You know what, I am fucking done here. Go screw yourself!" and with that, I walked out the door and slammed it, as he was bellowing my name.

On the other side of the door, I leaned my defeated body against the door for two seconds, willing the tears not to come. As I looked up, I swore everyone was looking at me. I swear, nothing was more embarrassing than that.

Slowly, I walked to my cubicle like I was being lead to the gallows with Michelle right on my heels. Why wouldn't this bitch leave me alone?

"Soooooooo Emma, curious minds would like to know, how you, of all people, landed Jerome McKinney Jr. I mean serious, Ems, look at you!" I glared at her.

"Really, what is that supposed to mean Michelle? Am I too ugly to fucking land a man? What is really your issue because I really don't have time for this right now."

"No it's nothing like that, it's just that you're…..well plain."

"Plain? Really. Well listen closely, I am two seconds away from ripping your perfect ass to shreds, so if you know what is good for you, you'll get the fuck out of my office, NOW!" I swear I do not know what to do with this girl; it is as if the farther from her I try to stay, the more she comes around! The fuck is her problem?

She laughed, the bitch had some nerve. "Why yes! He needs someone who he can show off and take to outlandish dinners. You know all that type of stuff…more ladylike. Plus, you will do no such thing." Oh, this is rich!

"Well Michelle, don't worry, I can hold my own, especially when it comes to sex. I have one question."

Without thinking, I pounced on the bitch, swinging wildly. Connecting every blow, so she did not have a chance. A crowd started gathering outside of my door, which sent me into a deeper frenzy.

When I thought I had enough, I left her slouched over crying on the floor. I had enough of her and everyone else. Of course, everyone knows. The office has been buzzing ever since he damn near chewed out the paramedic in front of the building. What the hell was I thinking that this would work?

I looked at her on last time before I grabbed my stuff and headed out the door. Jerome stood there in the mist of the crowd and the look on his face was one to remember.

"You're fired," that was good enough for me, but I had to create a bigger scene.

"No mother fucker, I quit!" Somehow, I was relieved and scared all at the same time. What am I going to do about work now? I mean, I can start my own practice. Yes, that is exactly what I will do. I went to my momma's house to get Izzy and started to get myself together for the long journey.

Chapter 6

In life, I guess everything has its good and bad periods and right now, I am going through mines. I had no clients after three months of setting up *Ross Inc.* and Jerome and I seemed even further apart. After our first huge argument and the fight at the office, Izzy and I spent two whole weeks with my parents, which is more time I ever spent with them, since I moved out the house.

The beginning of the third week, I said fuck it and headed back to the place that Jerome and I shared or so he thought. To my surprise, the house was relatively neat and the nanny was no longer there.

At my old job, I was basically the highlight of everyone's gossip hour. The hush tones could be heard every time I walked pass someone. Their eyes were all judging me when I went to pick up my last check from Jerome. What the fuck is wrong with people like seriously, did any of these people have a fucking life?!

It was ok because I was a strong black woman and I did not give two hoots about what was really the underlying problem.

The house has been quiet and I had to admit, I did miss how tight Jerome and I was, so I decided to tell him to come back home. Tonight, I am going to reach out to Jerome and I hope it works. Stopping at the store, I picked up a few things just before I grabbed Izzy. On the way home, I noticed a hot little number in the window of this new lingerie store that opened up, *Chic* something. I pulled in, quickly got my size and was gone.

It took me exactly two hours to put Izzy to bed, cook and get myself ready. At eight o'clock, I called Jerome, just as he came into the house. Calling my name, he followed my voice when I yelled that I was in the kitchen.

Coming into the kitchen, he stopped short, which was the exact reaction I was going for. Slowly, a smile crept across his face. This is something I have not seen since our first argument.

"What is this about? I came hoping that we can talk."

"It's nothing, just a little 'I'm sorry' present to tell you I want you to come back." OMG, I really do not think he knows what he is doing to me at this very moment with that sexy smirk of his!

"Goodnight Jerome, are you ready for dinner?" my breath hitched in my throat for a moment before he answered.

"So, because you say to come home, I am supposed to?" Shit, I did not know the answer to that.

"No, I am not expecting you to do anything. I was just asking if you would."

"Emma," he paused, "I need you to trust me. I need you to listen to me. You are the world to me, but I am not going to put up with this bipolar behavior like fighting in the office. Michelle was going to press charges, but I ask her not too!"

"Since when you're so fucking cool with Michelle?" My mood went straight to the left.

"What the fuck Emma? See that's that bipolar shit I was talking about!"

Before I even thought about it, I flung a glass straight at his head. "Bipolar?! Bipolar?! I'll give you fucking bipolar!" I started flinging everything in sight that I could get my hands on. "Did you ever consider my feelings in this whole shit, huh Jerome? No the fuck you didn't," another glass crashed an inch closer to his head.

"Emma. That's enough!" His voice boomed with authority, but I did not give a fuck. Whoops, there goes the plate. He had to dodge this one and with that, he reached me in less than four strides.

Jerome was angry. I clawed and scratched at him when he slammed me against the counter, bringing his large frame with it to pin me.

"Get off of me," I seethed.

"Not till you calm the fuck down!"

"And why the fuck should I? You treat me like shit and expect that I should be cool with it."

"I treat you like shit? Emma I been nothing but here for you. I can't believe that you would even think that!" Somehow, the mood turned from being pissed to all hot and heavy on Jerome's part. He was rubbing all on me and I could not think.

"Since dinner is all on the ground, I am ready for dessert, Emma," he drawled. With that, Jerome cleared the remainder of the things on the table in one swipe of his large hands and placed me onto it.

Slowly, his kisses crept up my neck and his hand ran sensual circles around my inner thighs. I could not help it when a moan escaped me. Jerome has always been great with his hands, but every time was like the first time. When he dipped his fingers into my ever-growing heat, my body automatically arched beneath his touch and a primal need took over.

"Please Jerome, stop," I moaned.

"Is that what you want?" I wiggled. I needed him, every inch of him. I burned wherever he touched. Similarly, his need was greater and he refused to let me take over.

"I can't wait any longer Emma, it's been too long." Swiftly, he positioned himself, ripping off my panties in one swift motion and filled me. This is what the hell I have been waiting for!

Moaning to the top of my lungs, I thank God that Izzy was a sound sleeper because it had been awhile since I had some of her dad. Kissing me tenderly, Jerome began to work his magic and I was so close to the edge. With every stroke came a response from me. I could not hold it any more.

"O...M...G... Jerome! Please baby right there!" I was a mess. The pain and pleasure of being with him was too much.

"Come the fuck back here, where the fuck you think you're going?" He was talking shit and I loved it. "You really think you were going to keep this pussy from me, really?"

"Oh fuck! Oh God!" By this time, I was grabbing and pulling at his shirt he still had on. He was close to climaxing and I was right behind him.

I started to breathe heavier and writhe and wiggle, I could not keep still. Just the mere expectation of what I know is to come raises my heart rate, widens my eyes and causes me to graze my teeth across his skin.

Jerome then brushed his fingers across my nipples, the soft pinch turning to a hard bite; exquisite pain sending electricity straight to my clit. The slow writhe and wiggle becomes an arched back. As the sensation of expectation increases, the greed for the explosion intensifies while he stroked the living daylight out this pussy.

My breathing became erratic, an uncontrollable moaning escapes my lips, and my heart beats faster, faster, faster. I pushed my body against his throbbing manhood, as his gasps came closer together.

My body exploded and I could hear Jerome moaning in ecstasy, in his release. I saw lightning bolts that seemed so real, so powerful, I can almost see them as my back arches violently up, and my shoulders pull back, as I cry out the name of God. As my pussy tightens and relaxes, again and again, the waves of sheer energy crash through me. Energizing yet depleting, each wave bringing us down both mentally and physically, until I slump, exuberant, yet exhausted.

As my eyes remain half-shut, my mouth curved into a feline grin. Words of love and desperate need and apologies spilling from my mouth, I feel as if I have finally reached where we need to be after being wound tight about the situations around us.

Quietly, we made our way to the bedroom. The

silence was deafening. We took a shower together, his hands all over my body, as he studied every inch of me. As we finally climbed into bed, the next thing out of his mouth completely shattered the fantasy that I had created.

"Sooo babes, I am leaving on the first flight to Atlanta in the morning," This motherfucker has to be out him mother-loving mind. Like really, Atlanta, after a night like this?

"Are you fucking serious, Atlanta, really, Jerome?" My voice probably went up an octave too high, but I did not give a hoot in a barrel at this point. I was tired. "What the fuck is in Atlanta?"

He looked bewildered, "What?"

"I said what the fuck is in Atlanta? Are you fucking some bitch down there?"

"Awe babes, don't be like that!

"Don't be like what Jerome? Every time I think that we are going somewhere or even getting back on track, you up and disappear again. What the hell is really going on?"

"There is nothing going on Emma, it's starting to sound like you don't trust me? This is outrageous!" Outrageous, I will show his ass out fucking rageous!

"Really? So, explain to me the logic of every time you come home, the next day you are going back to Atlanta? Being gone for almost a month every single time and I almost think, I am falling out of love with you."

I know, I know, how can one fall out of love? Well, it is plain and simple. When the person you love, whether it be man or woman, is doing the opposite from what you expect them to. Shit happens!

I got up from the bed that we were sharing, just looking at him in disgust. I was still lost for words. After everything we just shared and me, trying to work things out because I thought that maybe I was overreacting. Now, I was faced with this hard decision.

"Jerome, I am saying this once. This is hard for me to say because I love you very much, but it needs to be said. If you leave Izzy and I tomorrow, do not bother coming back." There I said it and I felt like a weight lifted off my shoulders.

With that, I walked out of the room feeling like the bottom of a barrel of rotting fish cum. It was a long time coming. For anyone that knows me, knows I am not the one to be put on the backburner and to make things worse, I have your child! Fuck out of here.

"Emma! Emma!" Jerome was shouting my name as I walked out of the room down the wooden corridor of our home to Izzy's room. I even sped up a little, just to give him a chase.

"What?" I asked as I turned the handle to the door and walked over to our beautiful creation.

"You couldn't really think you could give me an ultimatum like that and just walk away, what about what I have to say?"

"What do you have to say? Is there anything else to be said?" I knew it was childish.

"How could you even say that? This is us we are talking about. I feel like you are just finding reasons for us to be over. Is that what you really want?" I rolled my eyes. The truth is, I am trying to keep calm as I breast feed Izzy.

"I told you what I had to say already. I do not see the reason why you cannot work from your office here. All branches do the same work, and frankly, I am tired of doing this on my own.

"But you're not on your own, Ems. You decided you do not want the help!"

"Damn right, I did because YOU are supposed to be here being a father and helping with YOUR daughter!" Just then, Izzy started squirming in my hands because of all the noise.

"See, look what you did!" Jerome tried to take her from me, but the look I gave him, backed him off quickly.

"Move the fuck away from us! Make your choice, Jerome. I will no longer be a convenience to you. When you need me I am here, when you want me, I make myself available 24/7, but this, I won't be a part of any longer."

"I am leaving for Atlanta first thing in the morning," with that, I shattered. This is the end. He has made his choice.

"Don't come back Jerome, I mean it!" I shouted at him. The tears were rolling down my face by this time. He watched me with this saddened look on my face and closed the door to the room.

****

As the morning rolled in, the house was mighty quiet. At about six o'clock, I heard the front door close and a car driving away. I swear, a part of me died. I mean, like I was taken to a cliff and thrown into a sea of hungry sharks and just ripped apart.

I made my bed and now I have to live with it. I could not believe that he chose his job over his child and me. What can I say? I guess I am hard to love, but I made my decision. I was done with his shit. I was going to Atlanta and find out what the fuck he was doing down there.

Chapter 7

Within the week, I set up shop in Atlanta with Izzy in tow. I could not believe I had done this, but I needed proof to move on. Jerome hurt me and he knew he did, but he walked out anyway. If I find out he is fucking someone else, I will make his life miserable.

I walked into the *Regal and Ports* Atlanta branch first thing that Monday morning. I had to find the idiot of the bunch to give me more information. Bingo! I found her. She was a tall blonde, but she could babble all day long. I stood there for about five minutes in front of the receptionist desk, waiting for here to stop talking on the phone. Finally, when she realized I was in front of her, she hung up.

"Hiiii, welcome to *Regal and Ports*, how can I help you?" Ugh, I hated her already.

"Hi," I said with my best face on, "Where can I find Mr. Jerome McKinney Jr?"

"Oh, he is not in today. Actually..." She drawled, "He won't be in all week. It is his anniversary; I think he is taking the Mrs. on vacation.

I was deflated, but I got my answer. He was about to pay. He was married all this time and was setting up shop with me in Jersey, I am livid.

"Ok, thank you! Oh, before I leave, would you be able to give me his address? I have a very important message for him from the New York office." I worked at *Regal and Ports* for six years and I was not even sure if they had a New York branch.

"Oh," she paused, "I am not allowed to give out his personal information.

"Miss?"

"Kacey. I am Kacey Lowe," I smiled.

"Miss Lowe, I am sure that you are aware of Mr. McKinney Jr's temper. Personally, I don't want him going off on me when he doesn't get his information in time."

"Okay," yes, I whispered to myself, as she scribbled down an address.

"Okay, thank you Miss. Lowe. You do have a nice day," With that, I was out the door as quickly as I came. I hated Jerome. Right then and there, I made a vow that Izzy will never know what a lying cheating bastard her father was. He will never see her again.

As it turns out, Jerome lived about three blocks away from the hotel I have been staying at. As I looked at myself in the mirror, I watched the tears fall. It seems I have been doing that a lot lately. I was hurt just like any other woman would be. He used me and got me pregnant, now he is playing family man without me? Nah, it would not work. I had a plan in my head. It is time to execute it. I smiled at my tear-stained face and left on my mission.

****

I walked the blocks one by one, getting closer to his house. In truth, I was terrified but I was doing what had to be done. It is her. It was fucking her! My rage built up again, as I walked closer to the house. He told me he did not know her and I believed his dumb ass. Ugh!

She rounded the edge of the hedge of her beautiful home where she nearly ran me over. Recognition was instant, but there was another look, which she masked quickly.

"Darling, is that you?" yeah, she was good.

"Hi!! You live around here?" Yeah, but I am better. Turning around, she pointed at the house.

"Come in, come in. My husband stepped out to the store, but he will be right back," I smiled. Little did she know, I hope he does come through the door. I was hoping for the drop-dead look. I smiled and took a seat next to the baby stroller that held Izzy. I was wrong, I admit it for bringing her here, but I needed her father to see what he was doing.

Suzie was having a blast with Isobel when Jerome walked in. Bingo! The look on his face was priceless and the smirk on my face was real.

"Baby! Isn't the baby so precious?" she gave him a look, daring him to say something different.

"Good evening, sweetie," he walked over to her, placing a kiss on her forehead. "Who is this lovely young lady?" Oooo, I was two seconds from going off and if she sensed my plan, she gave me a look saying no, not yet.

"This is Emma, my dear. I thought you would know her. She works in your New Jersey office."

"Oh that's right! Emma how are you and want brings you to Atlanta?" I swear even the air around me stilled, as everyone waited for an answer.

However, before I could answer, Marie took the reins on the conversation. "No, I know exactly why she is here, but what I want to know from you, Jerome is how you could be so fucking stupid?" Her voice raised like ten octaves, even I winced at how shrill her voice became.

Before he answered, I cut him off. "So, I have been asking you all this time, what's going on

Jerome? Why are you always in Miami and Atlanta Jerome and all this fucking time you have a god damn wife?" he backed up out of the room.

"Get your sorry ass back in here!" Maria yelled. He walked back in like a little puppy. "So, I am figuring the baby is yours and you have been living with her while you're in Atlanta, correct?" He nodded. "So, who the fuck is in Miami?" My eyes opened on that one and I brought it up.

"You have someone else in Miami too?" I threw one of her pretty crystal glasses that was just decorating her table, and then I rounded on her. "You don't play fucking innocent!" I pointed at her, "You knew all this time and you couldn't even say 'Well bitch you fucking my man'!"

"Say what? When I saw you, I thought of you as a disappointment," Oh my god, I think I am going to go to jail tonight.

"A disappointment, really?" I could hear Jerome snickering in the corner. I threw another glass that whizzed pass her head. Warning number one.

"Bitch! Stop breaking those glasses! They are worth more than what you make!" Another one missed her by a hair, only because she dodged it.

"Who's going to make me, you?" I laughed, "Bitch please, you acting like it's all cool, but you can't even keep your dick at home!" The bitch swung and connected to my face. Shit hurt so much; I had to take a step back.

"Shit," was all I heard Jerome said before I blacked out on that ass.

"Jerome, get her off of me!" she tried her best to block every blow. As for Jerome, he moved quickly, taking our daughter into the other room while she screamed for help.

"Next time, keep your fucking hands to yourself! A disappointment?" I was about to punch her again, when Jerome pulled me off her.

"Emma stop it, that's enough!"

"Fuck off Jerome! Put me down, I swear I am going to make your life miserable. I got nothing but time on my hands!" I looked over at his wife trying to get up off the floor and laughed.

"As far as our daughter goes, you will never see her again," the background bitch started to laugh so much, she coughed.

"Didn't your baby daddy tell you?"

"Shut up Maria."

"For what, you let this fucking bitch coming into my house, break my things and beat me while you did nothing and I must shut up? I will do no such thing," She reached into her bag on the table and pulled out some papers. He dropped me as he tried to take whatever it was from her. "How did you think I found you, Emma?" she stated sarcastically. "He was planning on taking the baby from you girl. By the time he was done, you would have never seen her again." She threw the papers at my feet and I bent slowly to pick them up. Crack! That was the only sound in the room, as I punched him square in the mouth.

I was done. I was fighting and my mood was shot. I could not believe what he did to me and I thought I was the sneaky and conniving bitch. Well, I still am. I had a few more days left, but I think I will be heading back to Jersey tomorrow. That is when I noticed the bright red Ferrari FX in the driveway. I took out my keys and dragged it along the side of the car. I was mad and did not give a fuck. Did I mention, I really do not give a fuck?

I really could not do this anymore. The plotting and scheming behind my back, was too much. I was halfway down the block when Jerome came running.

"I'm sorry!" he grabbed my hand, pulling me to a stop.

"Sorry for what, Jerome? For being married or getting caught, which one is it?" He looked like a child being chastised for putting his hand in the cookie jar.

"What do you really want me to say? I have been married for ten years, we have our problems, but I could not leave just like that. Man come on!" He was starting to aggravate the hell out of me again.

"I asked you, Jerome. I fucking asked you about this. I asked you about her when she started coming around. You realize how much you been hurting me? It is me who looks stupid. It's me!"

He tried to hold me but I fought him off. "What you want me to do?"

"Get a good look at us because you'll never see us again," I started walking off.

"You can't be serious? Emma, I will fight you on this. You can't keep my baby from me!" I kept walking and flipped him the bird shouting, "Try me!"

The scene behind was one to be noticed. I barely looked back to see if Jerome was following me, but he was not. I pulled Izzy's stroller on the side to see if I could have a better look.

It was a 1995 Mercury black Max 150 rolling up next to Jerome. It almost looked like they were having a heated conversation, then the exchange of the briefcase. I could not look anymore. Whatever he was into needs to stay exactly that, what he is into, but it haunted my dreams for some reason. There should not be a reason that I care, but I do. At the end of the day, this was Isobel's father, whether I liked him or not.

****

I was back in New Jersey by nightfall the next day. I came, I saw and I got my answer. I did not need to find out anything else. Jerome is married and has an outside child. To make matters worse, he was trying to take my baby from me.

All day, he rang my phone. Leaving voice messages, trying to get in contact with me, until I turned it off. I needed to just move on. There was too much drama in my life at this point and here I am thinking it was me and I was creating things in my head.

As I looked around the house, I found there was no real reason to keep it, everything reminded me of Jerome. You know it was time to get rid of it. Should be simple enough, right? Right.

I sat down and reflected on my life. I was a single mom, no man and no job. I think I just hit rock bottom, but I will worry about that another day. Today, I will just relax with my baby and try to forget the events that transpired over the last couple of days.

It was about seven thirty at night when my doorbell began to ring, uncontrollably. I was not expecting anyone and I hoped it was not Jerome.

I shouted that I would be there is a minute. Why am I feeling like this was about to be some shit.

"Hey, can I help you?" I asked as I opened the door.

"Yes Darling, we need to talk," this bitch was at my door.

Chapter 8

"Hello Dear," I swore this bitch had this prim and proper air about her today.

"Hello and what can I do you for today?" I held my breath, because after the last encounter, I am not sure what she really wanted or why she was here.

"Well, it all depends," she trailed off for a second, and then looked at me to catch my attention.

"Well, can you please hurry? I don't have all day," I knew I was rude.

She then spoke very slowly, "Well, as you see, I am in a bit of a tiff at the moment." I looked at her.

"With what now?" Emma shut the fuck up, why you keep asking this woman questions. It is not as if you owe her anything! This was not good, I could feel it.

"Well, the thing is, it has come to my attention that my husband is back in this area. I would like to know where he is," I stared at her.

"Noooooo, noooo, noo, noo. I am not doing this with you. I do not know where he is, now have a good day. Get the hell out." This cannot be for real; this woman is up to something. Why me of all people? She wants me to help her find her no good philandering husband?

Lost for words, I started laughing insanely. By this time, she was just staring at me, "I know how hard it might be, for me to ask you for help, but please see it from my point of view." I looked at her face, for some reason, I could not say no. She smiled and squealed with delight. From there, we exchanged numbers and she left with a little pep in her step.

I do not know what the hell I just got myself into, but I think I will help her. She was a bitch, but the more I can hurt Jerome, I will. As I watched her retreating body disappear down the street of my house, I started to have large regrets about a lot of things in my life. I think today will be a pampering day. I should head out to the local beauty shop. Things need to start looking up because this life is not working for me at all. Right then, I made my decision to sell the house.

****

Within a half an hour, I got my mom to keep Izzy while I go and try to relax, just a bit. Walking into the nail salon, I ordered a Mani and Pedi. I could not help but overhear the conversations of two young women that work at a rival company, talking about what seemed to be, *Regal and Ports*.

"Did you hear? Jerome McKinney Jr. is selling out!" I pulled into a seat behind them, but tried to make myself unnoticeable until they were ready for me.

Wow, I could not believe that he was about to sell his dad's business. "You mean that hunk you had sex with during Christmas? Now, why would he do that?" Girl number two was a tall redhead that looked like she needed to be on the cover of *Vogue*.

Her partner in crime was a blonde but still just as beautiful. My heart ached; this day is really shaping up to be the worst ever. She giggled, "I overheard him talking to Mr. Roberts, our boss, about finalizing the sale of this branch. All the employees and everything should be turned over by Friday next week." I could not take the news. If I were there, would I have been out of a job?

Just as I was about to move, I heard my name. "How about the girl he has the baby with? I swear she is the biggest fool ever! What is her name? Umm Em...Em oh, Emma!" Blondie blurted out as if she just hit the jackpot.

The redhead started giggling. I looked down at my nails and tried to keep quiet. I mean, I know I am not the prettiest, but no one deserved to be talked about like this, much less, if you do not even know the situation.

Just then, one of the techs pointed to me to take a seat, so I sat next to Blondie. Of course, since

I was nobody, at least to them, the girls continued chatting about me and I smiled.

"You know Jerome told me he only kept her on because he felt sorry for her," I wriggled my toes in the warm water that the tech ran inside the tub.

"Really?! I thought you only slept with him that one time!" Blondie's grin spread like a Cheshire cat across her face. Jerome really knew how to pick them. I thought he was a black man in high society, yet he choose to mess around with these white chicks.

"No, we did it on a regular every night. For the past six months, he was never home! He told me he loved me, you know. I constantly told him to leave that old prune, but he didn't want to leave that adorable baby." Ok, that is it. They brought my baby into it and I did not like that at all!

"So, where is he now? He sounds like he was the love of your life," I knew I was goading her, but I did not give a fuck. I was sick of this.

Blondie turned, looked at me from head to toe and then replied, "He wasn't the love of my life, and he IS the love of my life. He has been staying with me, since he has been having a little tiff with his chick."

"Really?! Is that what he told you?" By now, the redhead is watching me as if I have two heads, but was mute throughout the whole interaction. I was grinning like the devil himself.

"Yes, I can't wait for him to come home tonight. I have a big surprise for him," Blondie started giggling again.

"Do you check out your surroundings before you speak Ms.?"

"Pollack, my name is Annie Pollack and what do you mean, if I check my surroundings? Everything I said was factual Ms.?"

"Ross, Emma Ross," I smiled as my name registered bells in her head.

"Oh my god...."

"Yes, oh my god. Personally, I do not give a flying fuck that you claimed to be with Jerome, but if you even utter my daughter's name or even my mother-fucking name anywhere, I swear I will hunt you down and rip that pretty little face of yours to shreds. Oh and by the way, Jerome no longer lives in the state of New Jersey, well he never did. He resides in Atlanta with his wife of ten years. I know, shocking right? It shocked me too when I found out, but I wonder Ms. Pollack, where do you get your information?"

With that, her face turned beat red and her friend pulled her away to the cashier to pay their bill. I sat back in my seat, as the tech started working on my feet. I didn't even know she overheard everything until she said, "Don't worry about women like that Ms. Every week she comes in here and she always has a different man living with her, so ignore her," I smiled at the tech. Maybe, it is time for me to make some hard decisions.

****

It was about one o'clock in the morning when there was knocking on my door. The first thing came to mind was something is wrong. I got my robe from in the bathroom and checked on Izzy really quick, then opened the door to find my mysterious stalker once again.

"It's one o'clock in the freaking morning lady, why are you here?" This bitch had better have a good… no, great explanation for this bullshit.

"I know, I'm sorry, but I have been following my husband all night and I didn't know where else to go!"

"So you came here? Why in God's name would you do that?" I was upset, but I was trying my best not to flip out on this woman.

"Child, don't ruffle your feathers," she spoke. This is a problem, I am way too accessible.

"What is it that you want, ma'am?" I was speaking through clenched teeth and I just wanted to go back to bed.

"I have no clue where I am. New Jersey is such a different place than the ATL. Can I crash here for the night?" I sighed.

"Ugh why? You know what, fine! Come in, just don't wake the baby," while taking her to the guest room, I peaked in on Izzy.

"She is beautiful, you know. We have been trying for years, but to no avail. Now, he has what he has been searching for," I saw the tears form in her eyes.

What was she trying to do, guilt trip me? "Jerome told me you have been married for ten years?" I knew it was a stupid move, but I had to figure out where she was going with this.

As she sighed, she stared at Izzy, "Ten years, we have been married, ten years and been trying just as long." My heart ached and went out to her. Ok, I really did not expect that one. Ten years and can't produce a kid? I would not wish that on my worst enemy.

"Would you like some coffee, Mrs. McKinney?" I did not know why I felt the need to hear the rest of her story, but I decided to anyways.

"Please, call me Maria" she smiled

"Alright Maria, let's get some coffee"

As the morning rose, she told me about her whirlwind romance to her husband. Right out of college, trying for the last decade to have kids and now, how the marriage is now deteriorating. Her story ended up with her here, in New Jersey. One of his colleges called and told her about me.

Now, here I am, sitting in the middle of my living room at almost five o'clock in the morning, listening to Maria go on and on about her relationship to her damn husband. OMG!! When will she shut the fuck up?

I went into the kitchen in disbelief that she even came to me trying to find him. Jerome was a whore and I did not need Izzy around him. Thinking on the scene I witnessed back in Atlanta, a thought occurred to me. I dropped the cup I went for in the kitchen.

"Is everything alright in there?" This time, she was in the doorway of the kitchen.

"Yeah, everything is fine, the cup just slipped out of my hand. So, what does Jerome do on his off time, Maria?" A girl had the right to find out, right?

"How well do you know him?" I paused before I asked, mentally going through a checklist in my head. I concluded that my sorry ass really did not know anything about him

"Well, it's obvious that I don't, but in any case, you wouldn't have to worry about me anymore. I am done."

As if it was a whisper, I heard, "It's not you that I am worried about, dear." This situation was getting weirder by the second. What in the world is Jerome really doing? I mean basically I answered my own question. It explains why he is always in

Atlanta, but it does not explain what I saw. I wanted to scream.

At exactly six o'clock, Izzy started to cry. Yay me! Saved by my silent alarm! It was time for feeding, but with Maria in the house, I did not want her to go snooping around the place to find anything that might remind her of my affair with Jerome. Coming out of Izzy's room, I found Maria heading out the door.

"You're leaving?" Yes, yes, yes, fuck yes. Do not mind me; I am having a party in my head.

"Yes dear. I have to catch a flight back to Atlanta at nine."

With that, the crazy bitch was out my door and speeding down the road towards the highway. Gathering my wits, I walked back into the house, shutting the door behind me. I looked at Izzy's little face as she laid on her blanket on the floor, kicking and blowing bubbles with her spit, with not one care in the world.

I wondered how her dad could be such a lying son of a bitch, but then again, it came easy for him. At about eight o'clock, the doorbell rang.

"Hello Emma." I swear to all God, if Izzy were not in my arms, I would have dropped her, as the shock took over me. He looked weary and tired. Jerome had come home.

Chapter 9

"You…you...You fucking son of a bitch!" Poor Izzy jumped in my arms. "Why the hell are you here?" Like really? This man has some nerve coming back here.

"Well, I do live here and I have decided you are not putting me out of MY house!" His emphasis on "my" made Isobel start screaming.

"This is not your house and you do not live here! You keep saying your house! You know what, you can have the house, 'WE' will be moving." As I turned to walk into the house, he grabbed a hold of my free hand and pulled me into him. It was too familiar, almost like his feelings for me were actually real. Emma! Snap out of it, start packing your bags and leave!

I pushed away, "I am leaving." Good girl!

"And where are you going to go? Back where? To your mother's? Please!" It was no ideal situation, but it might have to do, at least for now.

"Yes, back to my mother's house, but anywhere would be better than being here with you! Why don't you go back to your wife, she is looking for you." Even I cringed at that, but oh well; I have to be the bitch to get out of this one.

"Emma, what have I done to you?" Is this Negro really asking me a dumb question like that? I never turned around so quickly in my life. I thought I saw stars.

"What have you done to me? Are you fucking serious Jerome? Well, let us see what you have done. You were never here, you were always in Atlanta, but now I know why. To top it off, you are screwing everything that has a pussy and legs."

"Wait, what do you mean, I am screwing everything? I haven't been with anyone since you!"

"Really? Is that your final answer or would you like to phone a friend? Oh, how about you call Annie Pollack to help with that one!" Got him! He went quiet.

"How do you know about that?" His facial expression was priceless. Why me lord, why me? Don't I know how to pick them?

"Well, your little girlfriend had a nice long conversation with her friend in the nail salon and did not realize I was there. Now, you know what this week's biggest shocker was for me? YOU HAVE A MUTHAFUCKING WIFE!"

We had already made our way into the bedroom, where I placed a sleeping Isobel on the bed. I was pulling stuff from everywhere I could think of. I really cannot take this anymore; I refuse to be in something like this. I do not know what to do, but I think it is time for me to find my own way.

"I... I don't know what to say Ems."

"How about the truth for once in your pathetic life? How about I am sorry? But no, that is not your style. You do not have one ounce of decorum in your body to know what you are doing to all these women and me is wrong. I will not stay here and deal with it anymore. Now, if you excuse me, I want to finish packing up Izzy's room, so I can get out of here."

"Please, don't leave me Emma! I'll leave her, just give me that chance!" Oh God, please do not make me fall for the bullshit again.

"No, you wouldn't and if you do, who says you wouldn't do the same to me?"

With that, I picked up Izzy from off the bed and went to her room. As soon as I was inside, I locked the door. I never felt so stupid in my life. Here I am with a three-month-old baby in my hands and the man I loved on the other end.

****

It was a long drive out to my parents' house. I have always loved it out here, but because I was not compatible with my parents, I usually disappeared for long periods of time.

Coming closer to the house, the view of the beautiful landscape dominated by mountain peaks overtook me. My parents are not really, what you would call rich, but they were well off enough to afford the nicer things in life. As I approached the house, the rolling estate and dense woodland laced the hiking and equestrian trails. Oh, how I loved horseback riding. I wonder if Nessie was still around.

I was ready to spend the day laying by our private lake. I just knew Izzy would love it here, but will my sanity stay intact? That was the million-dollar question. Our family land was an extensive three hundred and sixty acres of farmland in Southern New Jersey. It was good to finally be home.

Inside, I found my mother cooking dinner. I placed Izzy in her little bouncy seat. We did not get along, but this was the meaning of home. It felt like home. Mama smiled at me, and for once in my life, I actually felt like I belonged here. Too bad, it took this to happen.

As the time flew by, my mother and I cooked dinner and cleaned the room where Izzy and I would be sleeping, at least for now. During this time, Jerome called like fifty times. I really wish he would stop calling! As I laid a sleeping Isobel in her playpen for the night, he called again.

****

Somewhere between panicking and me just wanting him to leave me the hell alone, I finally answered it.

"What the hell do you want? I need you to stop calling me!" I was through being a push over when it comes to him.

"Emma, we really need to talk." He was so smooth with it. I hate him!!

"Seriously Jerome, there is nothing else to talk about. I've tried and all you have been is a freaking liar from the start," I walked out of the room Izzy was sleeping in, so I would not wake her up again.

"Will you just let me tell my side of the story?"

"There is nothing more to be said! What more can there possibly be left to say?" Then I thought back, there was a lot more.

"Would you shut the hell you for a minute?" Shit that was rude. Humph!

"Fine, say what you have to say and never call me again."

"Yes, I was married, but I left her 6 years ago. Every relationship I have gotten into since then, she finds a way to rip it apart. It's just that this time, I have a child involved."

"Oh whoopee! Big shocker, Jerome the saint, right? Does this explain you cheating on me and talking about me to that WOMAN behind my back? Let me answer that for you, no it does not! I am sick and tired of being the puppet in whatever game that you're playing, but no more!" That actually felt really good.

I turned to look at myself in the hallway mirror of the farmhouse. I looked rundown; I was crying and did not even notice. At this point, my mother had already made her way upstairs, after I started yelling on the phone.

With a tender look in her eyes, my mom did not say a word, just engulfed me into her arms. This is why this woman is my superhero. I do not know what I would do without her.

After standing there for about five minutes of her consoling me, she told me she has a gallon of "Rocky Road" ice cream in the freezer and I was welcome to it. Like she really needed to tell me that twice. Sitting in the kitchen, she placed a spoon and ice cream in front of me and I went to town. Mom was there, just looking at me, so I knew what was coming next.

"How? I just have one question and that is how?" I groaned.

"Mom, can we not talk about this right now?"

"Young lady! You might be old enough to have a child, but I am still your mother and I asked a question. Now answer me, HOW?" The one person I have always been scared of is my mother, so I think it was best for me to answer her.

"Fine mom, it was a mistake that we tried to make work. That is about it. A one-night stand gone bad that left me pregnant and alone. To tell the truth, I was not sure if I would see him again. Then my boss died and there he was, riding in like Captain-save-a-hoe. I gave him a chance and he fucked it up, end of story," I breathed a little more slowly, but the tears threatened again. To make things worse, he was trying to take Izzy from me.

Just as she was about to speak, my dad burst through the kitchen door asking for his dinner. I smiled at mom and quietly slid out the kitchen because I really did not want to have this conversation in front of my dad.

****

The days seemed to mesh into each other. It was about two weeks before I actually started to job hunt again. Sitting on the roof, right outside my bedroom window, I felt a semblance of peace. I did not have to worry about Isobel at the moment because she was spending the day in town, with her doting grandmother. Just then, I noticed someone lurking around the back of the farmhouse.

Ok Emma let us think this through. Your mom is not here and neither is your dad. Where the hell are you going behind this shadow of a person? Calmly, I climbed back inside and got my dad's bat from in the kitchen. Slowly, I went around the back of the house and the figure, or should I say, young man was still behind there, reaching into his truck pulling out what seemed to be a tool bag.

"Who are you?" I thought about running into him like a mad woman, but this is Jersey. I am not trying to get shot.

As soon as he heard my voice, he turned around quickly, "Hey, hey, what are you doing?" Truth be told, I am not sure what the hell I was doing, but I was not going to tell him that.

"I asked a question? Who are you?" I looked at him more closely and to my dismay, my hormones started to go haywire. Just my fucking luck, he was sexy as hell.

"I'm Michael. I do small odds and ends jobs for the people that own the place." That calmed me a little bit.

"Oh...." What? That is all I got for now.

"Oh? That is all you have to say is oh? Hmmm, this is very interesting and you're pretty."

Ok, this was taking an interesting turn and I was not too sure on how to handle this. Putting down the bat, I relaxed and leaned slightly on it. "You're not too shabby yourself. I'm Emma...Emma Ross," I said while I extended my hand, introducing myself.

"Oh, Joseph's daughter," he said while he circled me like a vulture. "Joseph never said he had such a pretty little thing walking about."

I smacked his greasy hand away from my face as he reached for me, "He probably knows why he never told you." I said in disgust.

"Well, he probably thinks I would want to screw your brains out and if that was what he was thinking, he is right." Confident much?

"Aren't we the confident one? What make you think I would want you?" I had nothing else better to do. It was about two o'clock in the afternoon and no one was due home for another three hours.

"I'm not confident, I just know my skills and if I said I want you, I will get you."

"So what are you going to do? Force me to have sex with you? Right, that makes a lot of sense," my breath hitched, but I stood up for the challenge. If he tried anything, I still had the bat in my reach.

He laughed, "No honey, there will be no need for that."

"So, with your perception, how will you ever be able to get me to spread my legs for you?"

Maybe I should not egg him on; before I get myself into another situation without finishing the one, I am already in. Quickly, he spins around and pinned me to the truck, kissing me senseless. "This is only part one," he breathes between kisses.

Chapter 10

My body was on fire and I was not sure what else to do. The last time this happened, I ended up pregnant and alone. Maybe, this really is a bad idea, the last time I did this it was …. Damn his lips, oohh!

Umm Michael, please! His hands roamed all over me and I could barely concentrate.

"I told you, I get what I want and what I want is to taste every inch of you." This man was so damn cocky, it is ridiculous. Little by little, my resolves melted and I decided to give up the fight. I had not had sex since Jerome and I needed a release. Fuck it, might as well.

The Lord knew what he had planned for me because I had on my plaid schoolgirl mini skirt. His hands were quick reaching behind me as he pulled open the small door at the back of his 2014 Toyota Tundra truck. A sick sweet smile spread across his face and I imagined everything that he would do to me. "I am going to wash my hands really quick, I don't want that pretty little skirt of yours dirty." If you really know what I want dirty right now, you would stop teasing me.

I blew out a strangled breath as I watched him walked away, then placed my fat ass on the back of his truck and waited. This was not me. Bitch, if you do not stop trying to psych yourself out and get that dick. Just as fast as he left, he was back and he ignited the fire all over again

"Mind if I tasted you?" Was that a trick question?

"Baby, go right ahead," I lean back, baring my bald pussy covered in a bright yellow lace thong. He laughed and dove in between my creamy caramel thighs. Pulling my silk yellow thongs to the side, he started licking from my clit down to my inner core.

"Oh... My...God! You like that? Baby, you taste so fucking good!" My only response was a moan as he slapped his tongue on my clit.

As he eased my leg higher and higher into the air to gain more access, I wrestled against the oncoming wave of pleasure. Ok, at this point in time, I will admit. His head game is off the chain! Quickly, he pulled me to the edge of the truck, ripping my thongs off along the way. Michael had that rough sexual aura about him and I welcomed it.

Behind me, I heard the ripping of a condom wrapper. Thank God. A smart one. I also heard him opening his zipper preparing to take me. "Seems like you came prepared for this sort of thing, I can't help but wonder, if you didn't have this planned already?" He laughed and slammed home.

"I'm always ready for anything baby," I moaned again. He was definitely thicker than Jerome was and I could not help the moaning. I welcomed the painful pleasure, while he gripped my hands, holding them in place behind my back. Another earth shattering orgasm took over me, making me feel every sensation straight down to my toes.

Just as I was about to whip around and stick his dick in my mouth... oh my, it was gorgeous! I heard my dad's 2011 Ford truck speeding up the path to the house. "Oh shit!" I quickly started to fix myself and hide my torn panties. There was no way I would have made it to the house on time to hide in my room.

"What's wrong?" Michael was still in a daze, as he started putting himself together.

"My dad is home earlier than I thought! I knew this was a bad idea," he laughed.

"Scared of daddy, huh? Wait, how old are you?" he asked jokingly.

"Well, it doesn't matter how old I am, in his house, he will kill you!" I think that caught his attention. Shit, shit, shit! I kicked my ripped yellow thongs further under the truck as he walked up.

Knowing my dad, he surveyed the scene that was in front of him, as he walked up the path to where Michael and I were standing.

"Good afternoon, both of you. Michael, I see you've met my sweet Emma." He leaned over and kissed me on my head. Oh my god, I just want to get in the house and into my bedroom.

"Hi daddy, yes we have met. I thought he was a trespasser at first, but he is a good person and hard worker from what I have seen," Michael smiled. If this boy does not stop looking at me with this star struck look in his eyes!

"Well, I must be off! It was nice meeting you, Ms. Ross. Mr. Ross, I will see you tomorrow. My wife is cooking a big dinner for my birthday tonight." The bottom of my stomach fell out and my mouth opened. See! This is why I keep telling you to keep your fucking legs closed, Emma! Fuck!

"You tell Millie hello for me, will you?"

"I will, goodbye now," Michael took off and I forgot I kicked my thongs under his truck. There was the bright yellow silk just watching my father and me in our faces. With that, he walked off, leaving me there to stand on my own.

As you can tell by now, my life was spiraling out of control and there was no way to get it back at least that is how I feel. I just had sex again with a married man, my dad is pissed at me and I think it was time for me to move on. I have not even been back at the house for a week and I have gotten myself into trouble. I was starting to feel like a twelve-year-old girl again and I promised myself, this would never happen again.

Boston, MA…

Police Chief Commissioner Press Release.

Tuesday 16th June 2015

Police commissioner John Philip states they are investigating the suspicious death of a Boston Senator. Senator Frederick S. Milton, whose body was found, floating in the pool of his Victorian Boston Home, was pronounced dead. His death is being ruled as a homicide.

Spokesman Sgt. John Philip stated late Thursday evening that police do not believe that the death is connected to the string of high profile murders that has been taking place throughout the state of Massachusetts.

———

Friday 26th June 2015

Police allowed several days to pass before announcing the capture of Senator Fredrick's killer, Senator Kevin Lovett of Franklin County. They are hereby asking the media to refrain from being anywhere close to the crime scene.

As many lined up to protest the arrest of the Franklin county senator, one man was placed into handcuffs after walking up to the police and yelling at the officers for several minutes, for no apparent reason.

A curfew was put into place earlier this week, to keep the citizens from interfering with investigations, after protests called for the release of Senator Kevin Lovett.

****

Looking out the window of my cell, I feared my days were numbered. Whoever was doing this to me was doing a great job. I fought for my people, I would lay my life on the line for them, but they claimed, I killed my best friend. Senator Franklin Milton aka 'Frankie' grew up like me, on the wrong side of the tracks. We lived in the same neighborhood actually, until his mom married big and they moved into the suburbs. However, Frankie never forgot about me. Now, he is dead.

"Hey Lovett, you have a visitor!" The prison guard yelled from three cells down, like I could just walk right out of my cell. Patiently waiting for a guard, I hoped to God that it was Jerome McKinney

Jr., so we can go over all of my recent acquisitions. We needed to hide enough money in a Swiss account before the FBI gets a hand on this case.

I felt like I was walking to my death and I did not even know why. This case was ridiculous and they blamed me for it. To make matters worse, I could remember that night. I breathe of relief hit me when I saw Jerome sitting at the little table in the visitation room.

"Hey Lovett, how are you feeling?" He shook my hands that were still in handcuffs.

"Hey, I'm the best I can be," this was the truth in all honesty. "Did you bring the documents I requested?"

"Yes," he replied, while pulling the documents out of his briefcase.

"I can't believe this is happening. I have done many things in my life, but murder is not one of them. How much is in my personal account?" My mind started turning.

"Let's see," he browsed through the papers he brought. "You have about fifty-six thousand dollars in that one, about three million hidden in the savings account and another forty-five thousand in your offshore account in the Cayman Islands," I pondered on this information.

"I want it all moved, but I don't want any traces of it being moved. End of story. When this shit is over, I still have my monies to walk away with. I have worked too hard, for the life I live, for it to come crashing down on me. Now, there is something I need to ask you. I know you personally do not deal with criminal charges, but is there anyone that you know that can help me?" I waited for him to answer.

"Yes, yes I do actually, but I am not sure if she will answer my phone call." A smirk overtook my face.

"Really, a woman that doesn't do what the great Jerome McKinney Jr. says?"

"I know, right?" His laughter barked throughout the quiet room, "Well, she is one of the best lawyers my dad had at his firm, but she quit after my dad died. I ashore you that she would be the best person for the job." He spoke with pride and I automatically took notice, but I left what needed to be said, unsaid.

"Get her to Boston, Jerome. I don't care how, just get it done," he smiled, and then announced that he would get right on it. I never doubted his wisdom. I knew he was the right man for the job.

****

It has been three whole days since dad spoke to me. Mama asked what happened, but I refused to tell her. Everyone was quiet around the table when my phone began to ring.

"Can we just have quiet around the table, please?" Dad snapped at me. I just raised my eyebrow and slowly pushed my chair back, removing myself from the scene he was making.

Secured in the other room, my phone continued to ring. I hope this is a call about a new job. I took a breather and answered, "Hello?"

"Hi! Is this Emma Ross?" The lady on the other line sounded way too perky for my taste.

"Yes, this is she..."

"Great. Well this is Emily Shy from *Morgan and Ritts* in Boston, Massachusetts. I'm calling to inform you that you have a meeting with Mr. Claudius Smith for two o'clock tomorrow afternoon."

Yes! Yes! Yes! I started to do a mental jig in my head, "Of course, I will have to leave early, but I will be there!"

"Awesome, I will let Mr. Smith know that you will be on your way so we can book your room," I paused. Book a room? What kind of job is this?

"Room?"

"Yes ma'am, I am not allowed to say, but I will ease you mind. This is more than an interview. They are actually hiring you on the spot. You came with great references from a close friend of his." Okay, I will take that.

I squealed, "That is great. I am on my way then!" Emily laughed on the other line.

"Pack for about a week, then we will get you settled!" With that, she was gone.

I walked out the room back into the dining room and picked up Izzy, who was in her bouncy chair next to mom. I started spinning her around, sending her into fits of giggles.

"And why are you so happy?" My mom asked, trying to stifle a laugh.

"Cause she's a damn fool, that why," I shot daggers with my eyes at my dad.

"Anyways, I was just offered a job at *Morgan and Ritts*! I am excited and have to go pack. Mom, will you be able to watch Izzy for me for about a week? Pleeassssee," I gave her my best puppy dogface.

"Fine, I will. Where is the job? Why do you have to pack?" She inquired as she took a giggling Izzy from me. I was still making funny faces at her.

"It's in Boston mom."

"Honey, I am so proud of you!"

"I wonder who you had to sleep with to get this job," daddy said. What?

"Excuse me?" I was praying I heard wrong.

"You heard me!"

"Joseph!"

"Why are you being such a fucking dick? I didn't have to sleep with anyone!" I was furious. I took his verbal abuse for years, but I am not about to sit here at almost twenty-eight years old and let him continue.

"Because my daughter is a fucking whore, that's why! My daughter lets any and every man jump in between her legs and never thinks of the consequences." Well, there it is. I know what my father thinks of me, now I am good.

A sad smile spread across my face, "Well, you don't have to worry about your little whore anymore; I'm fucking done with you. I will be out in less than half an hour and I will be back for my child in a week's time."

"Good, but heed my warning Emma. You're going to get yourself into some serious trouble if you don't slow down, you have a daughter."

"What does my daughter have to do with it? Any who, that's not your problem anymore, is it?"

With that, I walk out of the room, packed my bag and was out of his house in exactly half an hour. A new journey awaited me in Boston; I just did not know where it would lead.

Chapter 11

That night I cried all the way to Massachusetts' capital. By the time I reached the hotel room Emily prepared for me, it was exactly twelve o'clock in the morning. Exhausted, I flopped across the bed. A gut feeling settled in my stomach that things were about to change. I knew it. It is just sad that my parents, once again, will not be here to see it.

About eleven o'clock the next morning, I got up and ready. My room in the Hilton overlooked part of the city and the excitement started to bubble. It was late August by now, so the heat was bearing down on me. As if on cue, my phone began to ring.

"Hello?"

"Hello, Ms. Ross, how are you?" the male voice was a deep baritone, but nothing much to make me excited.

"I am great, thank you for asking Mr.?"

"Mr. Smith, Mr. Claudius Smith," He answered with a chuckled. "How are you enjoying Boston so far?"

Well Senor Dipshit, I have not gotten to explore yet. "Oh it's beautiful! I never have seen any place like this!"

"Ok, that's great to hear… well, listen Ms. Ross, I know I told Emily two o'clock this afternoon, but will you be able to come to my office now?"

Checking my watch, it was about a quarter to twelve, "Yes, sure I can to that."

"Great! A car will arrive shortly to bring you in." As soon as he hung up, right on cue, the car pulled up and I got in. The driver looked old enough to be my grandfather, short, fat and balding, but that did not stop him from smiling. I could not help but smile back.

"Good afternoon young lady, beautiful day isn't it?" I smiled.

"Yes, it really is."

"All set and ready to go?"

It sounded like a loaded question, "Ready as I'll ever be."

It took about twenty-six minutes to get to Lexington. We had about ten more minutes until we reached *Morgan and Ritts,* so I pulled out my phone and started googling the history of this city. It reminded me of a place where a war happened long ago.

Lexington was first settled circa in 1642 as part of Cambridge, Massachusetts. What is now Lexington was then incorporated as a parish, called Cambridge Farms, in 1691. This allowed them to have a separate church and minister, but was still under jurisdiction of the Town of Cambridge. Lexington was incorporated as a separate town in 1713. It was then that it got the name, Lexington. How it received, its name is the subject of some controversy. Some people believe that it was named in honor of Lord Lexington, an English peer. Some, on the other hand, believe that it was named after

Lexington (which was pronounced and today spelled Laxton) in Nottinghamshire, England.....

I continued to read more from Wiki and was in awe. People who really know me, knows I am a major and I do mean, MAJOR, history fanatic.

As the car jolted to a stop, it pulled me out of my daydream of the newfound information, "We are here!" My driver announced. The butterflies surfaced again. As my driver nodded to me and drove off, I headed to this large antique heavy door, which I assumed was the entrance. Right behind the desk was a perky blonde, no more than eighteen years of age.

"Emily right?" I know one should never assume, but she looked like an Emily. Really Emma? How does one look like a name? It was a long shot but I had to ask.

"How'd you guess?" She was bubbling with laughter, "Come with me, Ms. Ross. Mr. Smith is in the conference room waiting on you."

As I walked into the room, the hairs on my neck stood up. I have not seen or heard from him in weeks, but he is here, in the conference room that I was about to enter.

Quickly, Mr. Smith wrapped up whatever they were speaking about and said their goodbyes. For a brief moment, I felt him brush against me as he passed through the door while I was on my way in. I stiffened at the touch, but tried to keep a straight face for appearance.

I took a deep breath as I took my seat and Mr. Smith started speaking, "Ms. Ross, I will get straight to the point. After the glowing review you got from one of my friends, we have decided to hire you and get you straight to work. Will that be an issue for you?"

I was stunned, I must admit, but I welcome the challenge and the new job. "No, no issues at all! Thank you so much!"

"No, Ms. Ross, thank you." With that, he handed me a medium size blue binder. "I need you to start reading up on your first case. I'm not going to go into details, but we need to win this case." Damn, first day on the job and he is making demands. Shit!

"Ok, no problem. I will get right to work," he signaled for Emily.

"Take Ms. Ross to HR and get her a desk. Welcome to *Morgan and Ritts*, Ms. Ross." I was full of glee with my job and my first assignment. The day moved by with a blur going to HR, with filling out paper work to be paid. It was exhausted.

As I sat at my new desk, I glanced over the file in front of me. Senator Kevin Lovett, I looked over the passport-sized mug shot within the folder. He was a total hottie, but I had to cool my loins on this one. However, the things I would do to him, if he were not a murderer.

So, let me get this straight. Best friends, one murdered and the other's fingerprints all over the crime scene, covered in blood, and he said he did not do it. Honey that is red flag 1, 2,3,4,5 and 6!

First things first, we need to find something, so he can make bail and return to his normal life until his court date. It took me two hours of combing through the case with a fine toothed comb, but I found it, nevertheless.

In the first statement taken by Boston PD, Senator Lovett stated that he could not remember anything from that night. He was on his way to meet with Freddie, but made a detour to a bar over on Congress Street, and then he blacked out. Something was not right and I have found the missing link, but I just hope it was not too late.

It was about six in the evening when I eventually slid out of the office. I was tired, but I needed to call my mom to check on Izzy.

"Mom, how are you?"

"Oh Emma! Give me a second, let me place the food on the table for your father," I cringed on the mention of my father, but I did not call for him. "Ok, I'm back. How are you?"

"Mom, I am great. I have a new job where they are paying ninety grand a year plus benefits. I got my first assignment today, so I am doing my best," I could hear the excitement in my mother's voice.

"Baby, that is awesome, I am really happy for you. What's your big case I saw on the news, that they arrested the senator for murder?"

"That's the one, mom. That is the exact case that was handed to be today and since its so high profile, I can't talk too much about it," mom paused on the other side.

"Listen, I don't like this murder stuff, but I'm not going to stop you from doing your job. I will keep Isobel until you finish this project though."

"But mom!"

"Don't but mom me. I will not let you be involved in something as dirty as murder and have you taking care of this little girl." It was the end of the conversation with mom and I could hear my dad agreeing with every word.

"Fine mom, fine. I will miss my baby."

"I know you will baby. You work on your case, and then come for her."

"I pray this don't take too long. Goodnight mom."

"Goodnight baby." It was always good talking to mom, I mean she always gets her own way, but it was always great.

****

"Is she here?" I was back in the small cubicle they call a visitation room.

"Yes, she is here and getting settled. I threw a bone to an old partner of mines and now, she is permanently working and will be living in Boston," I smiled

"Great! I hope she is as good as you say she is."

"Trust me, she is."

"Did you get done what I wanted you to do?"

"Yes, everything is set, moving it out in small increments, so it doesn't raise a red flag within the system."

"Great man, that is just great. I want to thank you, Mr. McKinney, for all your help." As I said this, I rose to my feet and shook his hand.

"It's my pleasure Senator Lovett."

As I was escorted back to my jail cell, I said a silent prayer. I, personally, will not do well in here, so I try to stay away from everyone else. In all honesty, the place was creepy.

Two days later, my prayers were answered and I was released from prison on fifty thousand dollars bail. All my travel documents were taken away, to keep me from fleeing the country. As I stepped outside, for the first time within three weeks, a vision stood in front me with two cups of Starbucks coffee in hand.

"Senator Lovett?"

"Who's asking?" She pondered her next move, but her poker face was horrible. I watched a million emotions and thoughts cross her face within a second before she answered.

"My name is Emma Ross. I am your new attorney," I smile, so this is her?

"Ahh yes! I have you to thank for getting me out of jail!" she laughed, which was such a pleasant sound to here.

"Yes, that would be me. Well, I do have a car here waiting if you would like to follow me."

"Do I have a choice?" She smiled.

"No, not really," And with that, she walked off.

The view was great. I never had the trouble landing the woman I wanted, but being locked up for three weeks with no tail does damage to a man is limbo. Man! She looked no more than five feet eight with that smooth milk chocolate caramel complexion and the perfect ass. Looking like a damn peach, I would just take a bite out of that...

I was pulled from my thoughts when a short balding man stepped out of the car and greeted her.

"Afternoon ma'am." I swear I lived in Massachusetts all my life and I could never get over how they stressed their 'A's'. I was glad to be out, that was all I cared about. I knew shortly that they would announce that I would no longer be acting in my post as Senator until this case is solved, but my freedom that is all I care about.

As we got in the car, I could not help but ask, "Are you married?" There was that tinkling sound again.

"No...No, I am not Senator. Why?"

"Please, call me Kevin. If this case can't be solved, I don't know how much longer I will be a Senator."

"Well Kevin, I am doing my utmost best to see what can be done, but there are so many unclear areas."

"Like?" I could not help but challenge her.

"Like, what happened when you stopped off at *The Drink* and why were the next twenty-four hours so unclear for you?"

"Your right. You know I have racked my brain so many times trying to remember what happened but nothing comes. I remember a tall blonde my accounting attorney set me up with. I promised to meet her, which I did. We talked, I went to the bathroom and blacked out," she just nodded and started jotting down everything I told her.

"So your accountant, who is also a lawyer, what's his name?" I paused for a second and looked at her beautiful face.

"His name is Jerome. Jerome McKinney Jr. We have been friends since college and he has stuck with me ever since." Maybe it was just me, but her body language changed dramatically for an instant, but disappeared as fleetingly as it came, "Do you know him?" I was curious.

"Yes, I am familiar with his work," she smiled, but it did not reach her eyes, like the rest of the times she laughed or smiled.

"Ok great, you guys should work together great," I was probably missing something here, but I would not force the issue at this point in time.

My life changed for the worst almost a month ago, but I am hoping this beautiful young woman and my one of my longest known friends would be able to help me.

Chapter 12

Sitting across from the Senator made me feel dirty. Wait, not in the way you are thinking. My woman parts were screaming touch me and he was Jerome's friend. Is it bad that I am fantasizing about him? Ok by now, you are thinking I am a whore and even now, I am convinced that I am. So right here, right now, I making a pledge I am not going to fuck this man, no matter how sexy he looks in a suit.

My mind was off in left field somewhere when he asked me a question, but I did not understand what he was saying.

"Helllloooo."

"Huh?" I looked up from where I was writing.

He smiled. There I go again! Stop it, stop it, stop it! "I was asking how you did it." His face was solemn.

"Did what?" I swear I was slow at times.

"I mean, how did you get me out of jail?"

"Oh that."

"Oh that," he mimicked then scooted closer to me.

I do not know, but the ride seemed extra-long today. Weren't we heading to my office or to his house, so he could shower and change? I really could not remember. He looked into my face and asked again, so I felt obligated to reply.

"Well, there were some inconsistencies with the paper work and procedures at the Massachusetts Correctional Institution. There were many black holes to your story."

"What type of inconsistencies?"

"Like for instance, they found you passed out covered in blood in your apartment. They didn't even do a toxic screening," I pulled out some of the crime scene photos. "Also, look here," I pointed to the picture of him. "You and the chair are covered in blood and there is no other trace of blood anywhere else in the house. However, you were covered from head to toe in blood. It makes no sense."

Grabbing the photo from me, he scanned over the scene, "Is there any way we can get the case thrown out?"

"Not as of yet. I called them on some of their bluffs, but hey, they are holding strong. They want hard concrete evidence." He grabbed my face and looked at me with a hungry look. I swear he was about to kiss me.

"Do you believe I did it?"

"Honestly, I don't. Based on all the evidence, it's not solid; the pieces do not fit together."

"I feel great that, for once, someone believes me. I don't know what it is, but as you can see, I am not taking this very well." He sat back into the chair with a brooding look on his face. I felt even more compelled to find out what was going on. The good thing is that mom has Izzy until this was over, but I pray it was over soon.

Right then and there, I decided that I was going to *The Drink* to have a talk with the folks over there. The ride to his house was longer than I expected, but when we arrived to the property, it was breathtaking. I watched in slight awe, as we drove through the wrought iron gates with the ornate leaf design, which opened on their own accord, as if invisible hands pushed them along their way.

The grass smelled freshly cut, and was immaculate; drops of dew were clinging to the blades of grass like little encrusted jewels. All around us was a garden made from flowers and plants that looked like they belonged in a travel brochure instead of this garden. A fountain gurgled merrily before us, water spraying from the always-smiling cherubs' jars and pots.

Kevin snorted at the flowing garden and scowled, "Those idiots!" he muttered angrily under his breath.

"Excuse me?" I asked, genuinely confused as to why he would be angry. It was so beautiful and lavish here.

"Isn't it obvious? Those stupid landscape artists I left to trim my garden has ruined it! Now I don't know how I will ever get this fixed in time for my party."

I could feel my eye twitch, why that conceited, bratty, little gave me a look that said, "Don't even think about it." I pouted, but my anger quickly disappeared upon sight where Kevin lived. I could feel my jaw drop to the floor.

There were at least five floors and the thing was wider than two of my schools put together. Ivy crawled up on one side, and rose bushes and other scented flowers grew around its edge. Intricate stained glass adorned nearly every window, and there were spirals coming out of it, like a castle.

"It's considerably small, but I do hope you like it," Kevin said, a smug look at my expression.

"Small? Really? You call this small?" I was still in awe. Ok, girlllll, he got freaking money! Sorry, that video clip popped into my head at the last minute.

He laughed as I mentally shook the image out of my head, "Come in and see the place."

"I don't think that I should," I was genuinely not sure if I should go, but he held my hand and pulled me out of the car behind him.

What was waiting for us inside was ten times different from what I was expecting. His things were thrown everywhere. The couch that he was found on was removed. Broken glass was everywhere and his office was ransacked. It brought him back to reality on what was going on around him.

Without a second thought, I pulled out my cell phone and called the police. Something was definitely wrong here and I was not about to let him go into this situation alone. Within ten minutes, the police were there, combing the area for any new clues. Whoever came into the house took the chair.

Now what would a criminal want with a dusty old chair? This is getting weirder by the second.

"Are you ok?" His voice interrupted my thoughts.

"Yeah I'm fine, I should be asking you this question?" He paused.

"This is worse than I thought and I don't even know what it's about."

"We will figure it out. You just bought yourself some extra time with me. Somehow, I feel we have to do our own investigative work."

"You sure you want to be seen around a criminal like me?" He stepped closer, so no one heard what he said. Quickly, I slipped away from where I was standing, before he could get a hold of me.

"Trust me, I can handle it. I think I have found a way, so we don't have to get too involved in the case," He contemplated what to do next, with the words that I just spoke.

"Ok, I'll bite. What should we do?"

"A private investigator," He smiled.

"And I know exactly the one to go too."

****

Within an hour, the police cleared the vicinity of Kevin's estate and we were on our way. Since I am new to the town, the scene changed quickly in front of my eyes. I was quiet as I stared out the window, but I felt his eyes on me the whole time.

"Tell me about yourself."

"Huh?" I knew I heard what he said, but I was not too sure, why he asked me that question.

"Tell me about yourself," he repeated.

"I am not too sure if this is a great idea."

"Of course it is. The car is quiet and I would like to get to know my lawyer more," I produced an audible breath.

Ok, let me stop this real quick. Good girl! "This is my first case, at a new job and personally, I don't think we should take this any further than it is."

"And where is it? Honey, all I ask you to do is tell me about yourself. I don't see any harm in that unless you have something else on the brain..." his voice trailed off.

I turned and took a real good look at the man that was sitting next to me. He was more sophisticated with that distinguished look about him. His hair was also beginning to grey, salt and pepper sprinkled across his head, which indicated to me that he was much older that Jerome. I sighed, that name popped into my head again and it was enough to kill any mood I was in.

"Fine, I will tell you about myself. I am twenty-eight and a mother of one beautiful little girl. I used to work at *Regal and Ports*, but I quit a couple of weeks ago and I was lucky enough to find a job that upgraded me....." For the rest of the drive to wherever he told my driver to go, he asked questions and I gave answers. I must admit, it was fun, just talking. No more than that.

We pulled up to an open area on Fenwood Road in Boston. Right in the middle of the space was a wooden shack that looked like it was slapped together. Kevin knocked on the door.

"Yo! Who is it?" A high squeaky voice came from behind the door.

"Rabbit, it's me!" He peeked out the door that was barely cracked open.

"Rabbit?" He shushed me. Wait, did he really just... Nooo, he had better not! I quieted.

"Heyyyy, well isn't it my senator himself!" They went into their whole macho man routine, while I just stood there shaking my head at them. "So! Who's the pretty lady?"

"Hey, hey hands off man, this one is mine," I am guessing this man did not get the memo yet. I did not answer, just shook my head again. Rabbit left the door open as he went back to his worn lazy boy armchair. Kevin turned to me, speaking very quietly.

"Listen to me well, Ms. Ross. I always get what I want and I meant every word I said, you are mine. I will have you," With that, he walked off, leaving my knees weak. I really do not understand these men. How will I work with this man? Ugh!

Walking into the small space, I met the men conversing. About what I really do not know, but they stopped as soon as I parked myself next to Kevin and gave him that look. Well, I was not too sure if he took it another way because the look that I got could have ripped my panties off.

"Anyways," he responded. "Rabbit, we need you special expertise."

"Oh yeah?" He cracked his neck all in one motion.

"Yes, I am kind of in a bit of a bind and if I don't find the culprit soon, I might be heading to jail myself," I swear this man has a voice smooth as honey.

"Wow, Mr. Goodie Two-shoes in trouble? This is somewhat hard to believe. What do you need my help for?"

"Have you seen the news lately?" I jumped in, before Kevin could reply.

"Yeah, yeah I think so. They have been going crazy about that murdered Senator they found in his pool.... NO FREAKING WAY! It's you they got for that?"

"Bingo!" I replied. "Also, on the day of his release from prison, we found his house ransacked and his couch missing."

"You think it's all connected?"

"Going with my gut I do, just like I feel that he did not commit this murder."

"You got a lot of confidence in old Lovett here."

"Yes I do and I do believe we will solve this case."

I started pacing the room, "So what do you want me to do?" Rabbit asked again.

"I've heard you've done great investigative work."

"I am one of the best!" I swear I saw his little scrawny chest puffed out with so much pride.

"Well, we need you to find out more info about what is going on. We will do some snooping on our side."

"Wait, isn't the cops supposed to be doing all of this stuff?"

"Yes, just make sure you don't get caught." With that, I walked out the door, leaving the guys speechless. I felt fearless but it was time to call my baby. I took all of five minutes on the phone, updating my mom partially on the situation. Leaving her pleading on the other end for me to be safe, the last thing I told her was to kiss Izzy for me and I will try to run away to see you soon.

Chapter 13

As we slid back into the car, Kevin made sure he was right under me. I swear I could not think straight when this man was around. Listen here buddy! Please keep your dick inside your pants and off my back. I stiffened at his touch.

"What's wrong? I haven't done anything yet."

"How about we just talk about the case?"

"How about we don't? My home should be ready for my annual fundraising gala tonight, how about you come with me?"

"No, I don't think that is a wise idea, really Kevin."

"Why not? It is perfectly harmless. We don't even have to call it a date." That smile again. Within the same instance, he pulled my legs so I ended up on my back. Oh my God! What is he doing?

I swore I saw that little bald headed man in the front, grinning from ear to ear in the mirror. Slowly, he laid down on top of me, making sure I felt every inch of his chiseled body. Instantly, I became self-conscious thinking of every mark that the baby left.

"What are you doing?" I tried to give a firm push on his chest, so he can move off me.

"I want you to just feel what you do to me."

"Ok! We need to set some ground rules," I swear this man is strong as an ox; I just cannot get him moved! "I am your lawyer and I cannot have you screwing up my job. Thank you very much, so please, get off of me."

"Not until I do this..." Within that same instance, his full lips came crashing down on mine. I have felt many things in my lifetime but this was new. A warm fuzzy feeling took over, from the crown of my head, shooting towards my feet; I started to lose myself when the car pulled to a sudden stop.

"Please get off of me."

"Say you will go with me?" I contemplated his request again.

"I have nothing to wear." He planted another quick kiss on my lips.

"That can be arranged. I know a lovely young lady that just opened a new boutique called *Rosé*, she imports very lovely dresses. You should go there. We start at eight- thirty sharp."

****

The store was beautiful and I still could not believe I was making this move on actually attending this function with Kevin. Me of all people. I am in no way, shape or form ready to take on the elite.

Walking over to a beautiful champagne colored gown that was covered in Swarovski crystals, I was in love, but the price tag was something different. That was not going to stop me from at least from trying it on.

"Can I help you ma'am?" I jumped, probably squealed a little bit, as a really tall brunette approached me.

"Yes, I would like to try on this beautiful dress."

"It is lovely isn't it but I think you would like this black one over here." She led me over to the fifty percent off rack. The dress was nice, but I wanted to see how my creamy chocolate colored skin would look against that material.

"No, I would like that dress," I pointed to the dress back on the mannequin.

"No, I don't think you can afford that."

"Excuse me? Miss, I do not know if you know how the chain works. I ask for the dress, you give it to me. You do not ask me if I can afford it. You ask what size," I was heated and I was very close in creating a very bad scene within the store.

"I don't answer to you. I give you what I think you can afford. Lady, act your wage," with that, she turned her back on me. Just then, another young lady, about the bitch's height but blonde, really beautiful with flawless porcelain skin, appeared from the back.

"Excuse me, are you the manager?"

The lady walked over to me, where I was still standing next to the dress, "Hi yes, I am actually the owner." She extended her hand to shake mine.

"Great, I was sent here to your beautiful store by Senator Kevin Lovett," I was talking extra loud, just so the bitch in the corner could hear and soak in every word.

"Oh! You are Emma! Welcome! Nicolai, can you get Ms. Ross a glass of champagne?"

"I want to try on that dress," I pointed, once again, to the champagne dress I was standing next to.

"Of course, what size are you?" She circled me like a vulture, "Oh I got it. You're a size two!"

She disappeared quickly and returned with the dress, then ushered me into the nearest dressing room. Five minutes later, I was nestled with the expensive fabric just staring at myself in the mirror. "Oh my God."

"Is everything ok?" she asked as she opened the curtains to my room. "Step out, step out, let me see! Oh my word, it is as if this dress was made for you. Now spin!" I felt like I was in a beauty pageant from how she had me spinning and walking about. About five minutes later, she found me a matching pair of shoes while I changed out of the dress.

"Ok Emma, we are all set. Just let me get everything into a bag for you and get you on your way. Is there anything else I can get you?"

Just then, Nicolai passed me heading into the back storage room, I supposed. "Yes, yes there is. Nicolai is it? I want her fired." I heard a frightened yelp coming from the back. Quickly, I ran through the whole ordeal and I never seen such horror on one person's face. Needless to say, I got my wish.

I was a bitch and I knew it. I could have let the whole shah bang go, but I could not. Checking my watch, it was about four o'clock in the afternoon. I decided to make a quick stop at the office hoping that they found me an apartment soon.

As I walked into my office about a half an hour later, "Ross, in my office now!"

Ewe that did not sound good. I wanted to drag my feet but I chose wisely not to, "Yes boss?"

"Have a seat. So, where we are on the Lovett case?" He was still chomping on a turkey sandwich, which looked nasty, in any case.

"I got him out of jail, if that is what you're asking," I proceed to give the details of my findings and about the break in at Kevin's house. I did my best to leave out the juicy details, so to speak.

"Ok, ok great work Moss!"

"It's Ross sir."

"Whatever." He waved it off, "Oh by the way, we have your new apartment ready for you to move in. It's fully furnished and all you have to do is move in."

"Oh this is great!" He handed over a key and wrote down the address. I was giddy inside. A new dress, I did not have to pay for and a new apartment, all in one day. Maybe, I will call my mom to see how my bundle of joy is doing. I do miss her. I do not know how anyone can do it; I cannot wait until she is with me one hundred percent.

****

It was about seven o'clock when I finally reached home, my new home. I quickly took a shower, which was needed after the day that I had and shimmed in my dress. Since I did not have much make up, I just put on a touch of lip-gloss and some eyeliner, the finish bringing out my almond shaped eyes. I looked into the mirror one last time, and then answered the door as someone began to knock. I wonder who could that be? There stood a man, would could have been as tall as Goliath. Okay I am exaggerating but he was tall and very well groomed.

"Hi, can I help you?"

"Are you Ms. Emma Ross?"

"Yes I am she."

"My name is Edgar and I will be your driver tonight to Senator Lovett's fundraiser. Are you ready?" He gave me an approving once over.

"Yes, just let me get my purse."

I was nervous. This was my first time being in such a high-class arena. I left the house about twenty minutes after I got home. How I did it, I still have no clue. I strolled through his front door about twenty minutes after eight and the party was in full swing.

I felt every stare as I walked through the crowd. It seemed to be a full turnout, but somehow, I felt that they were here out of curiosity. Like really, the man was arrested for murder and the whole town shows up to his benefit? It seems too weird to me.

I stood by the bar, I was still nervous and I need a drink to calm my nerves. When the bartender handed it to me, a familiar voice tickled my spine, to the point that the hairs stood on my neck. It is a shame that a relationship can go so sour. Well, mostly on my end, but still.

"I see that the city is agreeing with you."

"Jerome. What do you want?"

"Well, I can say you, but that would be inappropriate in the setting that you're in."

"How's your wife, Jerome?" I tilted my head to the left slightly trying to signal him to go away. I was really done with all his lies and refused to be a pawn of his anymore.

"How should I know? Probably lurking around here somewhere," He said as he waved his glass of champagne around.

"That's good for you, find her and leave me the hell alone." With that, I started to walk off, but he grabbed my hand and whispered in my ear.

"Be careful Emma, everything is not as it seems. Not everyone is your friend. You stick out like a sore thumb. Your little boyfriend, yes, I know about you all, was arrested for murder. Take care; you are being pulled into a spiraling world." He dropped my hand as Kevin spotted us and turned the other direction to a group of young ladies on the other side of the bar.

"Emma, you look amazing!" He turned me around to get a better look.

"Shhh, Senator you're making a scene!" I laughed as he kissed me on the check.

"Aww let them watch. I so want to kiss you right now."

"Oh no you don't, we have nothing. I am you Law-yer. We can't be seen canoodling in public." He pouted like a little school boy being scolded.

"Fine but you will be mines."

The night moved by slowly. I was introduced to Senator somebody and Governor something or the other, there were so many names to be remembered. All the while, Jerome stood in a corner and watched.

I kept my eyes on everyone. With this case, everyone was a suspect. I felt like I was quickly turning into Nancy Drew as I looked for clues in the body language of the people, but only Jerome keeps popping up on my radar. I pushed the nagging feeling behind me as I turned and smiled with the people around me.

At exactly eleven o'clock, the light in the building went out. There were incoherent male voices shouting and a single gunshot. Kevin held me close, as we lay on the ground, after the shot was fired.

"Bloody hell not here. Not now!" The light came on less than five minutes later, and then the screaming followed.

The Boston Globe

Police Chief Commissioner Press Release.

Thursday 10th July 2015

Police commissioner John Philip said it is a sad day within the Boston Community. Just weeks, after Senator Frederick S. Milton was killed at his Boston home, Governor Smith Jackson was found lying in a pool of blood at Senator's Lovett's annual Lionheart fundraiser. As police begins to gather more evidence, things do not look good for Senator Lovett. As the world looks, we are eager to see these cases solved.

―――――――――

We were back at the precinct and the officers were throwing questions left and right. Even I grew weary.

"For the last time, I did not do this!"

"He's right," I was tired of this and they finally let me, his lawyer, into the interrogation room.

"Ms. Ross., Detective Matthew." He shook my hand, "Can you verify his whereabouts?"

"Yes, he was with me. During the blackout, the gunshot went off and he jumped on top of me to protect me." The statement was short and simple. It got him out.

I know I would regret it, but I could not allow him to go back to his house.

"Until further notice, you are on house arrest. At my house."

"Your house?" His devilish grin was back.

"Yes my house. I hope that it will keep you out of the news for a while. Kevin, this is serious so enough of the games. Forget about us and let's get you sorted out because things are not looking good." He blew out a slow breath, letting everything I said soak in.

It was time to find whoever the murderer on the loose was and it's too bad, I have to play Nancy Drew to get this done. In the morning, I will head to *The Drink* and see where it will lead me.

Chapter 14

Well, maybe I should not have done this. I decided to hold off finding Rabbit to see what he knows. The day after the last murder, I took a drive over to *The Drink*, but I did not do any recon and speak to anyone.

I did this for the next month, so I can be known as a regular before I start asking questions. Today was no different. I went in and ordered my usual, a dry Strawberry Martini, and sat at the bar going through some of my hand written notes.

It has been almost a month since the last murder and still nothing. All he has been doing is lying around my house like a common beach bum. A sexy beach bum. It was getting to me. No matter how much I try to deny my attraction for the sake of my job, the nights has been brutal. Last night, threshold of my desire took flight and I rubbed an intense orgasm out of this world.

Sitting at the bar, a smile came to my face as I remembered last night. I hope he did not hear me through the doors. I need this case to be over with. Maybe then, I can get my groove on with him. I learned my lesson with Jerome and never again will I put myself in that sort of situation. Familiar voices entered the bar and I started laughing to myself. This man really think he had me for a fool. There was Jerome, in the arms of the same young woman he claimed he had nothing to do with during our relationship. I turned and took in the view before me. Did I feel upset? A little bit. Did I care now that I am fully aware of the situation? Hmmm no, I really did not.

When I thought I had enough of the scene, I paid for my drink and left the bar. Just as I was about to hop on the bus to head home, I felt someone pull me into his hard chiseled chest.

"Well lookie here! It's nice to see you Emma."

"Go find your whore Jerome. I need to get home."

"Yes, yes. I heard you have the Senator living with you now."

"First off, how did you know that and secondly, no he is not living there."

"Has he fucked that tight little pussy yet?" My God, he was fabulously annoying.

"No and why is that any of your business if he did?"

"Well, you have always been a slack one for the right touch," While he spoke, he ran his hand over my chest. Why was I breathing hard?

When I told you to leave, I was serious. Personally, I want nothing to do with you. Now go find your whore, I am heading home to cook."

By this time, thank God, another bus rolled up and I quickly hopped in so he could not speak. I am starting to feel like there was an ulterior motive to why I was in Boston and Jerome was behind it.

****

I was home safely and I was tired. Opening the door, the house was very quiet. I do not like feeling helpless. I need to get me a gun. I slowly walked in the house like a ghost. Where is he? By now, I was panicking, hoping that my meal ticket was not dead.

I found him on the couch, passed out. He was really a beautiful man. I walked to the closet and pulled out a blanket. By the time I came back to the living room, he was laying on his back. Covering him, he came out of his groggy sleep.

"Hey you," I smiled.

"Hi, you were in such a deep sleep. I nearly thought you were dead."

"Trying to get rid of me, are we?"

"No," I laughed, "Not trying to have you killed or rearrested yet."

"Yet?" He grabbed me and started tickling the living daylights out of me.

"Ok, ok I give," I was still laughing.

"Great!" He wound his hand in my hair. It felt so right and I hated it. I felt like this is where I was supposed to be, no, where I need to be.

I groaned, "How do you keep doing this to me?"

Trailing kisses down my neck, I gasped. "I seem to be doing a lot of things to you and I'm not even in the room."

"What is that supposed to mean?" I was curious.

His hot breath was tickling my ear, "How about I show you what you have been dreaming of every night since I have been here?"

In a swift moment, my banana republic pencil skirt was around my hips, while he started kissing on my thighs.

"Wait, we shouldn't be doing this," I pushed on his head that was still steaming hot kisses in between my thighs.

"You wouldn't be doing anything. Now relax and let me do what I have wanted to do since I met you."

I just could not deal, the pleasure that was pooling deep within my belly was becoming out of control. Just when I could not take it no more, he pulled my black lace panties to the side. Yes, I do have a thing for lace underwear. The first brush of his thick tongue was my undoing.

Firmly placing his thumbs in the space that connects my legs to my ass, he made sure I could not go anywhere, much less move, "Oh my God!"

"Let it go baby, I got you."

I was close to my breaking point and he continued to give me orders. I could not take it anymore; I broke when he slid two of his fingers into my hot dripping core.

"What… was… that?" I panted trying to catch my breath.

Then he placed a chaste kiss on my lips, I could taste myself on his lips. He laughed, "It's what I do best."

"Damn if that's your best…"

"Don't tempt me to take things further sweetheart."

"I'm curious now but I will leave this to another day."

"Oh before I forget, Rabbit called and said he got something."

Great. Finally, something I can work with. Maybe with more leverage, I can start asking questions at the bar.

"Did he say what he found? "

"No, he said to come over as soon as you got home."

"Sigh no rest for the weary," I got up and took a shower. The afternoon's events played heavy on my mind and I wanted more. I just hope that I can get him released for good.

****

About two hours later, we were sitting in Rabbit's small living room, anxious to see what he came up with.

"Ok ladies and gentlemen, let's get started." Rabbit was all-comical with it. He seemed to be very good at investigative work. If I was to guess, he was in the military at some point. Very clean cut although he was homeless, I mean looked homeless and almost could pass to be really handsome.

"Already, show us what you got."

"Well, I pulled the surveillance footage from your house and the bar during the week that you were drugged. If you would take a look here, you'll see where three men entered your house the day after you were arrested."

I kind of faded the information out as I stared at a form that was naggingly familiar to me. No, it cannot be. Could it? I decided to keep my thoughts to myself. There was no way in hell that he was part of this, but then again, it will surely explain a lot.

It took us about another two hours to go through the footage at the bar and at Kevin's house, but no one was familiar to him. I was stopped at any other avenue.

"Kevin let's go home."

"Ooooo, so are you two a thing now?"

"Oh no, no!" I interjected quickly before Mr. Senator could have answered.

"Really," He dragged every syllable out.

"Yes really and it is time to go." As I got up, a piece of gold paper stuck out of a pile of paper Rabbit brought over from the house.

"What's this?"

"What's what?" Kevin came up deadly close behind me to look over my shoulder. I turned to him

"This," I waved the paper in my hand.

Looking it over, a series of numbers next to the initials, FSM, was the first thing that caught my attention. Judging by the look on Kevin's face, I made a quick assumption.

"I guess you didn't write this?"

"Never seen it before in my life."

"I believe you. If I am correct, these initials are Senator Franklin's. As for the numbers, it can be a series of things." I handed the paper to Kevin.

"It looks like routing numbers for an account. You know what, I am going to call Jerome and let him look into it."

"No! No. Let me look into it. That is what I am here for," I took the paper back

****

Safely within the cocoon of my bed, I locked my door. Tonight, I would not be screaming his name. I heard arguing. I strained my hearing to catch what he was saying, but that was to no avail.

Whoever it was had Kevin really upset, but he reasoned in a very calm, but deadly voice. I dozed off in the middle of the argument, but at exactly twelve o'clock in the morning, there was a knock at my bedroom door.

"Waittttt."

"Emma wake up." His voice was filled with emotion.

"What is wrong Kevin?" This time I opened the bedroom door to let him in.

"It's Rabbit, Emma. He's dead," I could not believe my ears.

FOLLOW ME!

Facebook: www.facebook.com/AuthorRiivaW

Twitter: www.twitter.com/AuthorRiivaW

Email: riivawilliams@gmail.com

Website: www.riivawilliams.com

Mailing Address:

      P.O. Box 2001,
      Carrot Bay, Tortola,
      British Virgin Islands, VG1130

CPSIA information can be obtained at www.ICGtesting.com
Printed in the USA
LVOW10s1804160916

504963LV00017B/159/P